Into
the
world

BY VICTORIA EMERSON
AND JAMES J. THOMPSON

Illustrated by

J. EVERETT DRAPER

WOMAN'S PRESS
NEW YORK
1950

To Helaine,
Pat, Tommy, Hayden,
Dolly, Marcia,
Dick and Bill.

Printed in the United States of America
By American Book–Knickerbocker Press, Inc., New York
55

Into
the
world

Contents

CHAPTER I

Ellen makes up her mind

I̲T WAS JUST half-past three on a sunny afternoon. School was out and all the boys and girls were coming home. This was the happiest time of day for Ellen's little dog, Brownie, who sat waiting for her on the front steps. He watched other children run by and wagged his tail in a friendly way, but he didn't run down the steps. He didn't even bother to stand up.

Suddenly Brownie raised his ears, called "Arf!" and ran down the steps. Ellen was coming.

"Brownie! Hello, Brownie!" she called, running to meet him.

The little dog jumped up on her. He licked her hands, and wagged his tail so fast it seemed it must surely wag right off. Ellen laughed as she patted his silky head. "My goodness, you're happy today. Why are you so happy? Because spring is coming?"

She ran up the front walk with Brownie at her heels. She noticed the growing buds on the peach trees that stood on the side of the lawn.

"Yes, Brownie, spring is coming!" she laughed. "Spring is coming!"

"Arf, arf!" agreed Brownie, following Ellen into the house. Through the living room, through the dining room they ran. And then Ellen heard big brother Fred in the kitchen talking to Mother. Ellen and Brownie stopped in the doorway.

"Hello, dear," greeted Mother.

Fred stopped talking long enough to frown and say "'Lo." He was standing beside Mother at the gas range, talking to her as she placed a cherry pie in the hot oven. He stopped in the middle of a word. You could see that he was trying very hard not to show how much he liked cherry pie. But his tongue would not obey. It slipped out and licked the corner of his mouth.

Ellen looked up at her tall brother. "Looks awfully good, doesn't it?" she teased.

Fred looked down at her. "I don't care about pies, young lady. Maybe that's all you have to think about but I have other things on my mind. But you wouldn't understand that. Nobody seems to understand. Nobody!" To show he meant every word he said, he hit the hot gas range with his hand. Quickly he drew back his hurt hand.

"Ouch!" said Ellen.

"Arf!" said Brownie.

"Oh, dear!" said Mother.

"You're a big help—all of you," shouted Fred, blowing on his burn to cool it.

Mother got the butter. "Here, dear, let me put some butter on it." She took Fred's hurt hand.

"Oh, no, you don't," he said, pulling away. "That's

my hand, not a piece of bread. Stop trying to butter it!"

Mother looked hurt. Brownie looked with bright eyes from one face to another. He knew that something was wrong. In a questioning little voice, he said, "Arf?"

Fred was sorry. "Gee, Moms," he said, "I don't need anything on it. It didn't hurt that much. What really hurts is that you don't seem to understand me any more. I mean about Nancy and me."

"I understand very well," said Mother. "But I want you to finish college and be earning money before you marry Nancy."

"Oh, sure, wait till I finish college. Then wait till I start working. Then wait till I'm earning enough money. Then wait till I have a long white beard to trip over in church when I get married." He ran his hand through his black hair and growled, "Bah!"

Mother and Ellen laughed. "Anyway," Mother said, "if Nancy really loves you, she'll be willing to wait a couple of years."

Fred dropped into a chair. He stared at the kitchen wall as if he were seeing a dreadful picture there. "Two years," he whispered. "Two long years."

"You say that as if it meant two hundred years," Mother said gently. "Why, I waited three years to marry Dad, and I'd have waited ten if he'd asked me to." Then her eyes became dreamy as if she were looking at something far way, as she added, "Or all my life, I guess, for Dad."

Fred said, "That's just the trouble. Nancy is willing to wait. She thinks just as you do."

"Well, then, I guess that settles that. Nancy's a very smart girl," said Mother.

Fred didn't reply. He rose from his chair so suddenly he almost knocked it over. Then he stamped out of the kitchen.

Ellen made big eyes at Mother. "Whew! Some temper!"

"We have to forgive him," Mother said. "After all, he does have a problem on his mind."

"Yes, he wants terribly to marry Nancy, doesn't he? Do you think he will, Mother?"

"I suppose so. We'll just have to wait and see."

"I hope he does," said Ellen. "I like Nancy. I like her a whole lot."

"I do, too. I think Fred and Nancy would be very happy together."

Ellen seemed to be thinking very hard as she watched Mother take the cherry pie out of the oven.

"I wish I could think of some way to help them," Ellen said.

"Help them what?"

"Help them get married, of course."

"Why, Ellen, how could a little girl like you help them?"

"I'll bet you I will. Just you wait and see."

Mother stood still and looked at Ellen. "You're taking on a big job," she told her.

"Yes, I am. But I'll do it. You'll see." Ellen drew her mouth into a firm line and looked straight into Mother's eyes. Then she turned and walked out of the kitchen.

Mother placed her hands on her hips and stared after her. "I really believe she means it," she said aloud.

And Ellen did mean it. Yes, indeed. And when a girl like Ellen makes up her mind, well—things begin to happen! Just you wait and see.

CHAPTER II

Spring is here

"CHIRP! CHIRP!"

Ellen was awakened by birds singing in the cool morning air outside her bedroom window. She lay still and listened. Such a joyful greeting of a new day! She opened one sleepy eye and peeped over the top of the covers. Then she remembered it was Saturday. No school! Quickly she opened the other eye and sat up. Then she jumped out of bed and ran to the open window.

"Just wait, little birds," she called. "I'll be right out."

She pulled her nightgown over her head and threw it on the bed. Then she jumped into her clothes, brushed her curls, stepped into her shoes, and there! she was dressed.

The rest of the family were still asleep. Ellen tiptoed very softly down the stairs. Quietly she opened the kitchen door, and then she was in the back yard. The new grass was like a green carpet, and drops of dew sparkled everywhere in the morning sunlight. At the back of the yard were peach trees, so full of blossoms that their branches seemed covered with fluffy, pink snow.

"It's like a fairyland," thought Ellen. She ran to the

front of the house. There the weeping willow tree was gently swaying its branches, playing a pattern of silent music with sunbeams and with shadows on the bright new grass. The peach tree on the side lawn seemed even more beautiful than those in the back yard. All its blossom buds had opened into lovely pink flowers. Ellen ran to the tree and touched them. Mother and Daddy must be awake now. She could take a small branch of blossoms up to their room to show them. She bent back one of the tender branches and twisted it off. Then she ran into the house. As she bounded up the stairs she heard her parents' voices.

"Mother, Daddy!" she called. "Guess what I have."

Daddy came out of his bedroom. "Measles?" he laughed.

Ellen held the branch of flowers behind her back. "No, guess again."

She followed Daddy into the bedroom. Mother was slipping into her blue housecoat to go downstairs to prepare breakfast.

Daddy took his eyeglasses from the top of the dresser and put them on. "Let me see." He walked to the middle of the room where he could see Ellen's back in the mirror. "A branch of peach blossoms," he said very smartly.

"However did you guess it so fast?" Ellen asked as she brought the flowers from behind her back.

"Oh, I smelled them," Daddy wiggled his nose like a bunny. "But, Ellen, you know I don't want you to pick branches from our fruit trees."

"But, Daddy, they looked so pretty. I just wanted to touch them."

"Touch?" He took the branch of blossoms from Ellen's hand. "This is just a touch, eh?"

Ellen didn't know what to say. She just stood and looked up at her father. He continued, "And some of these might have made big, fat, yellow peaches for us to eat."

Ellen tried to picture the blossoms turning into peaches. She couldn't. "Just how do they turn into peaches, anyway?" she asked.

Daddy pulled a blossom from the branch. He sat down on the maple chest at the foot of the bed. "Well, now, that's quite a wonderful story," he said. "Do you want me to tell you about it while Mother cooks breakfast?"

"Oh, yes!" said Ellen. She sat down beside her father.

"A peach blossom has mother and father parts," he said, holding the blossom for her to see.

"Mother and father parts?"

"Yes. These are the father parts—these pink threads standing up around the center of the flower." Then he

touched the dark red tips at the ends of the pink threads. "Little tiny specks called pollen grains grow in these tips."

"But, Daddy," said Ellen, "all the threads aren't pink. The one in the center is light green, and it's longer and thicker than the others."

"The one in the center doesn't belong to the father part of the flower," said Dad. "It leads down to the mother part where the baby peach grows."

"Where's that?"

"Here—in the base of the flower." Daddy pulled off a few petals, took out his pocket-knife, and cut open the side of the base. Then he spread it apart. "Now, there's the baby peach. See?"

"A baby peach? Why, it looks like a tiny pussy willow, only it's pale green instead of gray. She touched it with her finger. "It feels like a pussy willow, too. And that's going to grow into a peach?"

"Well, it won't now. But if you hadn't picked it . . ."

"That's what I mean," Ellen said. "Then would it?"

"It might have," answered her father. "Of course, many of them fall off the tree before they become ripe.

The tree can't hold as many peaches as it has blossoms. And a pollen grain has to get inside the mother part first, or the baby peach won't start to grow at all."

"It does? Why?" asked Ellen.

"Inside the mother part there's a tiny egg waiting for a pollen grain. The pollen grain has to get to the egg and join with it to start the baby peach growing."

"But how can a pollen grain get inside the mother part?" Ellen asked.

"When the egg is ready for the pollen grain to enter it, a sticky liquid comes out on the tip of the green thread. Then when a loose speck of pollen lands on the sticky tip, it can't get away. It goes down inside the mother part to the egg and joins with it."

"Does it have to crack the little eggshell to get in?"

"Oh, it's not like a hen's egg," Dad said. "It has no shell. It's very soft and very tiny. It's made of only one single cell. But small as it is, the grain of pollen is even smaller. And it's just one single cell, too."

"A cell? What is a cell?" asked Ellen.

"All plants and animals are made of tiny cells that you can't see without a microscope. Your body is made of cells, millions of cells, all put together to make you. Every part of your body is made of cells."

Ellen looked at the skin on her arm. "It is?"

"Oh, yes, your skin, blood, bones, everything. This whole flower is made of cells, too."

"Oh," said Ellen. "And then what happens after the grain of pollen joins with the little egg?"

"They mix together and become just one cell. Then it

divides in half, making two. These two divide again, making four, and so on. In that way, many cells are made. And that is the way things grow."

"But what happens to the rest of the flower, Daddy—the petals and everything?" asked Ellen.

"The petals drop off. Then everything but the baby peach dries up. As it grows bigger it pushes the dried threads and base all up till it looks as if it's wearing a little cap. Then the cap drops to the ground."

"And the peach keeps on growing till it's big and fat and ready to eat. Yum-yum, how I love peaches."

"So you think the tree does all that just to give us peaches to eat?"

"Sure." Ellen looked puzzled. "Why else?"

Daddy looked at Ellen. "You think hard for a minute —and I'm sure. . . ."

Ellen thought as hard as she could. "Oh, I know," she grinned. "The tree does all that to make baby peach trees. The baby peach tree is in the pit, and when you plant the pit, a tree starts to grow."

"Right!" Dad looked very pleased with Ellen. "That's exactly right. When you plant the peach pit in the earth, the embryo in the pit—embryo means the beginning of a baby—starts to grow. It breaks through the pit, and sends its root into the ground, and its little trunk up into the air."

"And then it grows big, and gets beautiful with flowers, and makes more peach trees," Ellen added.

"Yes. And that's the way living things come into the world—from mother and father parts."

"You mean all living things?"

"Almost everything that lives and breathes," Dad replied. "Plants, chickens, fish, and other animals."

Just then Mother called that breakfast was ready.

"And we're ready for it," Dad called back.

Ellen followed her father downstairs.

"How would you like to visit a farm some week-end?" Dad asked at breakfast. "Ned Sanford's farm."

"Do they have horses?" asked Ellen.

"I'm not sure. But if they do, Ned Sanford would let you ride one."

"Ned Sanford," repeated Mother. "I never heard of him, nor his farm."

"Oh, I've known him for some time," Dad explained. "I met him downtown the other day and he invited us to spend a week-end at his farm. Ellen would like him. He's as jolly as a Santa Claus."

"And as fat, too?" Ellen asked, as she began to pile up pancackes on her plate.

"As fat as you'll be if you eat all those," Fred smiled.

"I don't care," said Ellen. "Please pass the butter, Daddy, and the sugar, and the cream, and everything to make me fat."

Mother laughed. "I think it would be fun to visit a farm," she said. "Someone please pass the bacon."

Dad was glad Mother wanted to go. "Memorial Day is on Monday this year," he said, "so if we go that week-end, we can have three whole days on the farm. Saturday, Sunday, and Monday. There will be no school Monday, and I won't be working either. I'll phone Ned

Sanford after breakfast and ask him if we may come out then. Someone please pass the jelly."

Someone did. "You'll come, too, won't you, Fred?" Mother asked. "Please pass the sugar."

"Pass this—pass that," Fred said. "Let's stop passing and start eating. No, I can't go that week-end. Nancy's family has already invited me to their summer house at the lake. We'll probably play golf. Someone please pass the cream."

"I know you can't break a promise," Ellen said. "Especially with Nancy."

Fred shook his finger at her. "See that you don't get into any mischief while you're at the farm."

Ellen made herself look very, very good. "But I never do get into any," she said.

"Well, then, it gets into you. And something tells me it's going right out to the farm with you." Fred folded his arms and looked at his sister.

Dad said, "Uh-huh, maybe you're right, Fred. But we can leave half the mischief behind if you'll promise to mind Brownie while we're gone."

"What? Me a dog-sitter?" Fred laughed. Then he said, "Oh, sure, I'll mind Brownie. I'll take him to Nancy's. I'll be very kind to him, too. If I get home first I'll even give him one of your best slippers to chew on."

After breakfast, Dad telephoned Ned Sanford and plans were made for the trip to the farm on the Memorial Day week-end. And what a week-end it was! Ellen will never forget it as long as she lives.

CHAPTER III

Ellen meets John

Iᴛ sᴇᴇᴍᴇᴅ a very long time for Ellen to wait, but the day came at last. Mother, Dad, and Ellen were up extra early, busy as bees, getting ready to go to the farm. Ellen loved every minute of it. She didn't forget to pack her western boots, either, because if there really were a horse on the Sanford farm it would be thrilling to ride him. Soon they were in the car, ready to go. Mother settled down beside Dad in the front seat and sighed with relief as they started off.

They rode along the highway through neat little towns and quiet country villages. Ellen sat on the back seat, looking out at scenes as pretty as painted pictures. They passed fields of green vegetables, houses built far apart, with distant hills and clouds like white cotton in back of them, big red barns and old gray wagons, churches with tall steeples, and horses grazing in sunny fields.

They came to a road that led over a hill, bringing them into view of a wide, flowing stream. They rode over a bridge and stopped on the other side so Dad could look at his road map. Ellen jumped out of the car and ran to the bridge. Cows were standing in the shade of big trees, grazing by the stream. Ellen could hear it bubbling over the large moss-covered stones near the shore. She leaned over the rail and saw how pretty the lower part of the bridge looked with patches of bright green moss growing on it here and there. When she raised her eyes, she saw that someone was watching her. He was sitting on the bank of the stream, fishing. A big brown collie dog was at his side. Ellen judged him to be a little older than herself. He had light hair, and a wide grin. He called "Hi!" and Ellen called back with a laugh and a "Hi!"

Dad got out of the car and shouted to the boy. "Can you tell us where the Sanford farm is?"

"This is it!" he answered. "I'm John Sanford." He scrambled up the bank with his fishing pole and string of trout, and the big collie dog beside him. As he came nearer, Ellen saw that his eyes were blue and full of fun.

"I'm Mr. Gordon," said Dad, holding out his hand. "And this is Ellen."

"Hi!" said Ellen.

John grinned. He patted his dog. "This is Champ," he said.

Ellen stroked the dog's fur. "He's pretty. I love collie dogs." Champ wagged his tail and licked her hand.

"Come and meet Mrs. Gordon," said Dad. "She's in the car."

John met her and then said, "Our house is down the road a little farther. I'll show you."

They got in the car and rode to a large old-fashioned farmhouse. Mr. and Mrs. Sanford came out to greet

them. Soon both families were together in the living room, talking and laughing like old friends.

John invited Ellen to the kitchen to see Melissa and her family.

"Melissa?" Ellen was puzzled, but followed after him.

"Sure. She's in there." John pointed to a basket in the corner of the big farm kitchen. There was a sound like a tiny motor boat coming from it. "What a loud purr!" Ellen laughed.

"Wait'll you see what she's purring about," said John.

Ellen walked over the bright rag rug on the wide board floor and looked into the basket. "Oh-h, aren't they cute!" She knelt down to get a closer look. "I'm going to hold one."

John lifted a baby kitten out of the basket and gently placed it in Ellen's hands. It had tiny pointed ears, a short pointed tail, and short little silky whiskers. "They're just three weeks old today," he said.

The kitten curled up in Ellen's hands like a ball of gray and white fur. "It feels so soft and warm. What's its name, John?"

"Oh, we haven't named them yet. Do you want to?"

"I'd love to." Ellen stroked the kitten, saying, "What a cuddle-cat you are. What shall I name you?"

"Cuddle-cat," exclaimed John. "That's a cute name for a kitten. Why not name that one Cuddle-cat?"

"All right," Ellen agreed. She placed Cuddle-cat back in the basket with its mother. Ellen took up another kitten. This one was almost all white, and its fur was very soft.

"How silky this one feels," laughed Ellen.

"Then we'll call it Silky," John said.

Ellen frowned. "See here, John Sanford. I thought I was going to be the one to name these kittens."

John pushed back his blond hair. "Gosh, I'm sorry. Let's begin all over again."

"No, thank you," said Ellen, taking up the last kitten. But, I'm going to name this one all by myself." It was white underneath, and tan on top. "You look like a toasted marshmallow," she whispered to it so John couldn't hear.

But he had, and he started to say, "Well, then, we'll call it. . . ."

"Oh, no," Ellen said quickly, "we shall not call it

Marshmallow, because I've already named it Whiskers. So there!"

John laughed. "All right. Whiskers. What names— Cuddle-cat, Silky, and Whiskers."

"They're very nice names," said Mrs. Sanford, walking into the kitchen.

"I like their mother's name, too," said Ellen. "Melissa sounds awfully pretty. What is the father cat's name?"

"I'm afraid we don't know that, Ellen. We keep several tomcats around the barn to keep mice away. Any one of them might be the father."

"But doesn't the father of these kittens ever come in to see them? Doesn't he know how cute they are?"

"No," said Mrs. Sanford. "He probably doesn't even know they've been born. Cat fathers don't seem to care much about their children."

"Oh, what a shame." Ellen bent over Whiskers in her lap. "You poor little cat, you! You have no father to love you."

Mrs. Sanford smiled. "Well, you see, Ellen, it's different with cats. A human baby needs lots of care from the time it's born till it grows up. That's a long time. And all during that time it has to have good food, clothing, a nice home, toys to play with—ever so many things that the father has to earn money for. And the mother has to stay home to take care of the children."

"Well, Nelly Ann has no father," said Ellen. "She's a girl who lives on our street. Her father died when she was a baby."

John said, "Then Nelly Ann's mother has to work

twice as hard to make up for no father. She has to earn the money and take care of her home and family, too."

"Oh, but it's different with Melissa," said Ellen.

"Yes," replied Mrs. Sanford. "While her kittens are small they drink milk from her, but in about a month they'll be weaned. Do you know what that means?"

"Well—not exactly."

"It means they won't have to drink their mother's milk any more. They'll be able to eat other kinds of food. Then they'll take care of themselves, too. They'll clean themselves, and drink and eat, without any help."

"I see," said Ellen. She placed Whiskers back in the basket. Melissa purred happily and lay down on her side. Her three little kittens came close to her. It wasn't long before each of them found a small pink nipple to drink milk from. They seemed very contented and so did Melissa. She closed her eyes, and she looked very smiley. Her front paw was laid quite tenderly over the baby cat nearest it.

Ellen looked at the little family and thought of what Mrs. Sanford had told her about father cats. Suddenly she said aloud, "Gee, I'm glad Daddy's not a cat."

John laughed, "I'll have to tell your father that."

Mrs. Sanford was leaving the kitchen with a tray of food. "Both of you come into the living room," she said, "and have something to eat. You must be hungry, Ellen, after your long ride, and we won't have dinner for awhile yet."

On the way in, John asked Ellen, "Can you ride a horse? Would you like to go for a ride?"

"Oh, boy, would I!" Ellen exclaimed. "I brought my western boots along. As soon as we're through eating, I'll get them from the car. I'll change to my slacks, too."

"Okay. I'll saddle the horses while you're doing that. Ma'll show you where your room is, where you can change. And then I'll meet you down in the stable."

John told Ellen how to find the stable. After they finished eating, Dad brought the bags in from the car, and Ellen changed to her slacks and boots. She found the stable all right, and as she went in she saw John with two very pretty horses.

"I got them saddled," he said. He patted the shoulder of the tall white horse. "This one's named Dignity. He always holds his head so high and proud, we figured the name suited him."

"It does, all right," said Ellen. "He's beautiful. And what's the brown one's name?"

"Sophie. She's gentle as a kitten. You can ride her."

"Gee, I'd love to," smiled Ellen, patting the horse's shoulder. "She has beautiful brown eyes, hasn't she?" She reached into her pocket and brought out some sugar squares for the horse. "I'll give Dignity some, too, in a minute."

Then they led the horses out of the stable and mounted them. "Let's go up and down the fields for a ride first," said John, "and then we'll go along the stream."

Up and down the fields they galloped, their horses' tails and manes flying. Later, they went down by the stream as John had promised.

The ride was over all too soon for Ellen. John took the saddles and bridles off the horses. "Gee, you're lucky to have a horse," Ellen said to John. "I wish I could get my father to sell his car and buy a horse."

John laughed. "Imagine your father riding to work on a horse."

They went back to the farmhouse. It was time for dinner now. After dinner, John told Ellen he had to do some work in the barn. Mrs. Sanford said she had to take care of the chickens.

"Oh, I want to see the chickens," Ellen said. "May I go with you, Mrs. Sanford? I can help."

"Do you know anything about taking care of chickens?"

"No, but you could tell me what to do. I'd love to help."

"All right," agreed the farmer's wife. "If your mother says you can."

"Of course," said Mrs. Gordon. "And Mr. Sanford is going to show us around the farm. We'll see you later."

"Come along then," said Mrs. Sanford to Ellen.

CHAPTER IV

A tree lays an egg

MRS. SANFORD, ELLEN AND JOHN all left the house together and went out into the sunny farmyard. As soon as John came out, Champ ran to his side.

"That's our cow barn over there," said John, pointing to a big red building. "And over there is the chicken house."

"What is that tall round thing next to the barn?" Ellen asked as they walked.

"That's a silo. It's full of food for the cattle. Chopped up cornstalks and stuff like that."

John left, followed by Champ, to go to the barn. Mrs. Sanford led Ellen to the chicken yard. As she opened the gate, all the chickens clucked and scattered.

"They know you're a stranger." Mrs. Sanford explained. "But come in here. You can see the baby chicks." She led the way into the large chicken house. And there, like bits of yellow fluff, were hundreds of tiny chicks running around under what looked like a small, metal circus tent.

"That's called a brooder," the farmer's wife told Ellen. "An electric brooder. It keeps the chicks nice and

warm. If they get cold, they'll die."

Ellen wanted to gather up a few of the fluffy little chicks. Mrs. Sanford told Ellen to make a nest with her hands and then she placed a soft little chick in them. Ellen was delighted. "Oh, Mrs. Sanford," she said, "it's so cute!"

"We're going to have more soon," Mrs. Sanford said. "Look over here."

Ellen followed Mrs. Sanford to a large cabinet. "This is an electric incubator," she explained. "Eggs have to be kept warm to make them hatch into chicks. The incubator keeps them warm day and night. I'm going to take some eggs out now—some that have been in here about a week. I'll candle them to find out which ones are fertile. John often does this work, but he's busy with the cows now."

"John knows how to do almost everything, doesn't he?" asked Ellen. "And he's so strong, too."

"Yes, we're mighty proud of John," Mrs. Sanford said. "I don't know what we'd do without him."

Then Mrs. Sanford removed a drawer of eggs from the incubator. Ellen followed her into a small dark room. The farmer's wife turned on a light in a thing that looked like a large tin can. She took an egg and turned it around in her fingers. Then she held it in front of the light and looked at it.

"This one is not fertile," she said. "It won't hatch into a chick."

Ellen was surprised. "Won't all eggs hatch into chicks if they're kept warm?"

"Oh, no," Mrs. Sanford replied. Then she laughed. "Do you think the eggs you eat for breakfast could have been hatched?"

"Yes, couldn't they?"

"No, indeed, they're not fertile."

"What's the difference?" asked Ellen.

Mrs. Sanford now had another egg in front of the light. "Here's one that's fertile. Look!" She showed

Ellen the egg with the light shining in back of it. It had a dim red spot in the center, and Ellen thought she could see some tiny red veins around the spot.

"That one will hatch into a chick," said Mrs. Sanford. Then she put the first egg back in front of the light, saying, "But this one won't."

Ellen looked at it. "It won't because it has no red spot?"

"That's right. It has no embryo. The red spot is the embryo, or the beginning of a baby chick. It starts as just one cell. That one cell divides in half, making two. Then those two divide in half again, making four, and so on until many cells are made. And the cells form into bones, blood, skin, feathers, eyes, and everything else that's needed to make a chick."

"But why does one have a baby chick beginning in it and not the other?"

"Because, before a baby chick can start to grow, the egg has to be made fertile by a rooster."

"Why?" questioned Ellen.

"Why? Why?" Daddy imitated Ellen as he and Mother entered the chicken house and stood looking into the dark room. "Has the Gordons' quiz program been bothering you, Mrs. Sanford?"

Ellen laughed. Mrs. Sanford said, "It's the smart children who ask questions."

This was fun for Ellen to listen to, but she hadn't yet been answered. "Daddy, why does the hen need the rooster to get baby chicks?"

"Well, you remember what I told you about the

peach blossoms, don't you?"

"Yes, but chickens aren't flowers, Daddy."

"That's true, but plants and animals both make their babies in about the same way," Dad said. "The rooster has to give the father part from his body. You remember this was called pollen in the flower? Well, it's called semen in animals. Instead of being dry, like pollen, it's a liquid with tiny things called sperm cells swimming in it."

"Are sperm cells like pollen grains?" Ellen inquired.

"They look different under a microscope, but they do the same thing. One of the sperm cells from the rooster's body has to join with the egg in the hen's body before the shell is formed around it. That makes it fertile, and after the hen lays it, it will hatch into a chick."

"Well, how do the rooster's sperm cells get inside the hen's body to make the eggs fertile?" asked Ellen.

"The sperm cells are in the liquid called semen. This goes from a small opening just below the rooster's tail feathers into an opening in the body of the hen. It's the opening the eggs come out of.

"Oh," said Ellen, "and after that, when a fertile egg is laid, it will show a red spot if you hold it in front of a light?"

"Yes, because a baby chick is growing inside it. So you see, Ellen, without the rooster . . ."

"There wouldn't be any red spots in eggs to turn into fluffy chicks. Why, Daddy, it's like magic, isn't it?"

"It certainly is wonderful," Dad agreed, "for a little living chick to come into the world that way."

"But what about the eggs we eat?" asked Ellen.

"Chicks would never have hatched from those eggs, because they were never fertilized by a rooster," said Dad.

"When farmers want eggs for market, they keep the roosters away from the hens," Mrs. Sanford explained. "And they let them be together when they want baby chicks."

"So you see, it's just like the peach blossoms," continued Dad. "A grain of pollen has to reach the egg . . ."

"To start a baby peach tree growing," said Ellen, proud of her knowledge.

"Exactly," agreed Dad.

"Well, then," Ellen went on, "a peach and a fertile egg both have a tiny—I forget what you call it—the beginning of a baby."

"Embryo," Dad supplied the word.

"Yes, an embryo. Only one turns into a chicken and the other turns into a peach tree."

"That's right," said Dad. "And a peach pit doesn't sprout until the following spring when the weather is warm enough to make it grow. And an egg has to be kept warm, too, to make it grow."

Ellen beamed. "Well, then, a peach tree lays an egg, doesn't it?"

Dad raised his eyebrows. "I never thought of it just that way, Ellen. But it's not far wrong."

Ellen watched Mrs. Sanford holding the eggs to the light. "How long does it take for a chick to hatch?" she wondered aloud.

"Twenty-one days," replied Mrs. Sanford. She was just putting back the last egg. "There, I'm through now. Out of the hundred eggs, I found that seventy are fertile. So we'll have seventy chicks in two more weeks. And now, Ellen, do you want to help me feed the chickens?"

Ellen was eager to help. She followed Mrs. Sanford while Dad and Mother returned to the farmhouse.

Ellen and the farmer's wife entered the chicken yard with bags of chicken feed and started to fill the long metal feed troughs. The chickens ran over, lined up, and began to eat as fast as they could. Ellen thought the birds very pretty—all snowy white with bright red combs and bright red beards.

Mrs. Sanford pointed out a few roosters. Their combs were higher and prouder than the hens', their beards were longer, and their tail feathers had a fuller curl.

"The roosters are prettier than the hens," Ellen remarked.

"Seeing how they strut, I'm sure they think so, too," Mrs. Sanford laughed.

"Yes," said Ellen, strutting about, imitating the roosters. "As if they're saying to themselves, 'Ho, I'm quite a beautiful bird, I am, I am. Yes, indeed, quite a beautiful bird.' "

The farmer's wife laughed at Ellen. "And now," she said, "if you want to see how cows are milked and fed, go to the barn and watch while I get supper ready."

"Gee," remarked Ellen, "there's an awful lot to learn about on a farm."

"Yes," answered Mrs. Sanford, "There's a lot to learn about how things grow. You see, Ellen, in the cities things are made in factories for people to use. But out in the country, farmers work with living things, plants and animals that make their own kind. Now, enough of that. I'm going to cook supper."

"Good," said Ellen. "I'm starved."

"You certainly look it," Mrs. Sanford laughed. "Why, you're almost as plump as one of my apple dumplings."

"I am not, but you are." Ellen looked laughingly up at her and took her hand as they walked toward the house.

"That's the price I have to pay for liking my own cooking, I guess. Just between you and me, Ellen, I'm the best cook in this whole county." She squeezed Ellen's hand. "And don't tell your mother and father I said so."

"Why not? They know it. Mr. Sanford told my father you're the best cook there ever was."

"He did?" Mrs. Sanford beamed, and smoothed her apron.

Ellen noticed how bright and happy she looked as she entered her old farm kitchen to prepare supper. Then Ellen walked toward the barn to watch John feed the cows.

CHAPTER V

Hortense is not a cow

Ellen entered the barn. John's father was carrying a shiny, stainless steel object. It was shaped like a big jar, with rubber hoses coming from the top.

He greeted Ellen. "Hello, are you going to watch the cows? John went for the herd. They'll come in any minute."

Ellen looked at the stainless steel object. "What's that?"

"A milking machine. You'll see how it works when we milk the cows," Mr. Sanford answered.

Then he told Ellen to stand out of the way against the wall. She stood by a pile of bags filled with feed—a pile almost as high as Ellen herself. Soon she heard the dull thud, thud, of many hoofs. They grew nearer, moving slowly. "Don't cows ever hurry, not even to dinner?" she wondered. They came through the wide doorway and walked over the clean concrete floor to their stalls. Then they put their heads through the stanchions, the long metal loops that keep the cows in place while they are being milked. John and Mr. Sanford hurried after them. They locked the stanchions as soon as the cows

34

had put their heads through to eat the food that John had set out on the other side. Then John, with a cloth and a pail of clean water, began to wash the cows' udders.

Now the cows were ready for milking. Ellen came over and stood beside Mr. Sanford. He connected a long hose of the milking machine to a pipe that ran along the top of the stalls. Then he turned to the first cow and put the four rubber-cuffed ends of the shorter hoses on her four teats, or nipples. The milker began to draw milk from the cow's udder. In a few minutes he moved to the next cow and the milker collected more milk. When the milker was nearly full, John brought a large shiny milk can and Mr. Sanford poured the warm milk

into it. Then John placed the cover on the milk can and carried it to the cooler, which was in a small room at the side.

"Gee, you're strong," Ellen said to John as she walked after him. "I couldn't even lift that thing, but you carry it as if it weren't heavy at all."

"It's nothing," said John. "I'm used to it." Then he took an empty can back for more milk.

"The milk is warm when it comes from the cow," John explained to Ellen, "so we chill it right away to keep it fresh. If we didn't, it would sour. Then we sell it to a milk company, and they pasteurize it before they put it in bottles."

Ellen listened and watched everything with interest. The barn was so clean, the cows were so pretty, and so gentle. Now Mr. Sanford was ready to move to the next cow. This one, Ellen thought, was the prettiest of all. She had noticed her when the herd came in. Her coloring was light-brown and deer-like. Her face was sweet as a doe's. She had long black eyelashes, and the brush on the end of her tail was black and silky.

"Oh, I like her!" exclaimed Ellen. "She's pretty. But why aren't you milking her?"

"Eh?" said the farmer as he moved to the next cow. "Oh, Hortense? Well, you see, she can't be milked. She hasn't any milk. She's not a cow."

"Not a cow?" Ellen wondered if Mr. Sanford really meant what he said.

"She looks like a cow." Ellen walked to the other side of the animal. "She looks like a cow from both sides, too.

In fact, she looks just like all the other cows, only she's prettier. And maybe her tummy's fatter. What makes her so fat?"

"She's pregnant."

"Pregnant?"

"Yes, she's going to be a mother," answered the farmer. "A baby calf is growing inside her right now. If you put your hand on her side, maybe you'll feel it moving."

Ellen did this, and a bright smile of surprise spread over her face as she felt the soft movements.

The farmer, too, placed his hand on Hortense's side and felt it. "Yep," he said, "that calf'll be here real soon now."

Ellen looked at Hortense. Just how does the little calf grow in there, and just how will it get out, she wondered. And also, she wondered why Hortense wasn't a cow. She was about to ask when the farmer began talking again.

"You see, Ellen, Hortense is only a heifer. She never had a calf before. She's a heifer until she has a calf, and after that, she's a cow."

"Is that why she doesn't give milk?"

John laughed. "Ellen, I guess you think cows make milk for human beings to drink," he said. "They don't."

"No?"

"Of course not. They make it to feed their calves. Dairy farmers just take it from them, that's all."

"You mean that when I drink milk I'm drinking food that was stolen from a baby calf?"

"Not exactly," Mr. Sanford answered Ellen. "Every farmer makes sure that his calves get enough to eat so that they grow to be big and strong. A good dairy cow makes more milk than her calf needs. And it isn't long before the calf is weaned, that is, before it learns to eat other food. But the cow keeps making milk as long as it is taken from her. That's almost up to the time when she's going to have another calf."

"I see." Ellen felt better about drinking milk.

"El-len!" Mother was calling. Ellen ran to the farmhouse. Mother was standing on the porch.

"I think it would be nice if you'd set the table while I help Mrs. Sanford in the kitchen."

Ellen was glad to help. Especially because someone else's dishes were different and fun. When the table was set Mr. Sanford and John came in. John told Ellen the milking was finished and the cows had been let out to pasture again.

For dinner, they had the fresh trout that John had caught in the stream that very morning. It tasted so good. Um-m-m! Ellen wanted to go fishing!

"I'll take you," John offered. "I'll take you Monday afternoon. There's going to be a parade over in Newton in the morning, but in the afternoon we can go fishing. I have an extra pole, line, hooks—everything you need—even worms."

"And will you show me how to bait the hook?" Ellen asked.

Mr. Sanford turned to his wife. "It looks as if you'll be cooking fish again Monday, eh?"

"Yes," Ellen promised, "because I'm going to catch dozens and dozens."

That night the two families gathered around the fireplace. Ellen and John popped corn. Mrs. Sanford sat in her rocking chair, knitting, and talking with the others.

"Fred would like this," Ellen said to John, as she watched him shake the popcorn popper over the flames.

"Fred?" asked John.

"He's my big brother. Didn't I tell you about him? He goes to college. He's learning to be an architect— learning how to draw plans for new houses. He's going to get married, too. Anyway, I hope he is."

"Why?"

"Because I like Nancy. She's wonderful. She's learning to be an artist, too. . . . Gosh! I hope they can get married! Anyway, I'm going to help them. Fred won't have a job for a long time, and Dad says you can't marry until you're earning enough money to set up a home."

"You help them?" asked John. "What can you do?"

"I don't know yet. But I'll think of something. I know I will."

"I don't see how a girl can do anything about it," remarked John. "Although you are pretty smart—for a girl!"

"Bedtime, children," Mrs. Sanford declared. "We go to bed early out here in the country because we get up so early."

They all went upstairs and Mrs. Sanford showed the Gordons to their bedrooms. Ellen's was at the end of the hall, right next to Daddy and Mother's.

Then Ellen washed, and brushed her teeth, changed to her nightgown, and went to Dad and Mother to kiss them good night. She went back to her bedroom and knelt beside the bed to say her prayers. While she was asking blessings for those she loved, her thoughts flew to the gentle, pretty cow and the little calf moving inside her. "And God bless Hortense," she added, and then climbed into bed.

How quiet everything was! How different from the city! The stars in the sky were like diamonds, twinkling on dark blue velvet. The moon was full and rising, filling the room with soft silver light. There was no sound except the voice of the night whispering through the trees, and the far-away call of a whip-poor-will. Soon Ellen was fast asleep and dreaming about fluffy little yellow chicks.

Suddenly she awoke with a start. Sharply through the night came the excited barking of a dog. A wave of fear swept over Ellen.

"Champ! It sounds like Champ!"

Ellen sat up.

What could it be?

CHAPTER VI

A prowler in the night

A DOOR OPENED very quietly somewhere. Then it closed very quietly. The sound of footsteps, as of someone walking on tiptoe, came to Ellen's ears as she lay awake and afraid, in this old farmhouse.

The barking had stopped. Everything was quiet again, quiet as death. Had it been Champ barking? Why had he stopped? Had someone hurt him or even killed him? Whose footsteps were those when everyone was supposed to be sleeping? She remembered something that John had told her: Champ never barks at night unless something is wrong. All alert now, she leaned on one elbow and listened. She heard more footsteps. This time they semed to be in the yard right below her window. Was someone trying to break into the house? Ellen got out of bed as fast as she could, and tiptoed to the window, and looked out.

The moon was high in the sky and it lit the roof and one side of the barn with a silvery glow. The black shadow of the barn made one part of the yard dark while the rest of it was bright in the moonlight.

Ellen looked out just in time to catch sight of something disappearing into the shadows. A man! What was he doing?

What should she do? Should she wake up her parents, or the Sanfords? She thought for a moment. Then she quickly slid into her slacks and shirt, and slipped on her shoes. Her parents were sleeping right in the next room. She would go—but—what was that? A footstep— in the hall right outside her door!

Her heart beat wildly as she stood at the door and listened. Then she turned the knob, carefully, opened the door very quietly, and looked into the dark hall. "Who's there?" she tried to speak, but no sound came out.

"Is that you, Ellen?" It was John's voice.

"Yes, John," she whispered, feeling better now.

"Did Champ wake you?"

"Oh, then it was Champ, wasn't it? Yes, I heard him barking." Then she told him of the other queer sounds, and of the man in the shadows.

"Let's find out what going on around here," said John, in a deep whisper.

"Hadn't we better wake up everybody?" Ellen asked.

"I can handle this," declared John. "You wait here. I'll get my flashlight. Something is going on around here, and I mean to find out what it is."

He felt his way along the dark wall back to his room. In a moment the beam of a flashlight came out of the doorway. John was in back of it. "Come on," he ordered.

As they tiptoed softly down the stairs, the old grandfather clock struck midnight.

When they were in the downstairs hall, John whispered, "We'll look through all the rooms down here to see if anyone is hiding."

They crept along the wall to the door of the living room, and looked in. Nothing could be seen in the silent darkness but the red dying embers in the fireplace. John told Ellen to stand back while he flashed his light around the room, and into the corners. Everything was in order as they had left it before going to bed. No one was in the room and nothing had been disturbed. Then they looked in the dining room, but everything here was all right, too.

They went on, creeping and shaking, to the kitchen. Moonlight was streaming in through the windows.

"Look!" whispered Ellen suddenly, grabbing John's arm.

"A light in the barn!" exclaimed John. "Who could be out there in the middle of the night? What are they doing?"

"I think we ought to tell your father," said Ellen, a little shakily.

"Nonsense," answered John. "We'll find out for ourselves. Come on!"

He went to the kitchen door. Ellen stepped in front of him. "Not out in that bright moonlight, John. They'll see you!"

John thought for a moment. "Let's go out the front door, and around the house. Then we can keep in the shadows."

They went back through the hall, opened the front
door and stepped out. John led the way around the
house.

"Now! Down behind the blueberry bushes," he
ordered Ellen.

They hid behind the blueberry bushes. The light in
the barn was still lit. Then strange sounds come from
the barn. And then a cow mooed.

"Someone stealing our cows!" exclaimed John.

"Call your father!" cried Ellen.

"No, they'll get away! Come on, I'll get them!"

John and Ellen crept along the row of blueberry
bushes toward the barn.

"Don't make any noise," warned John. "We'll look
in through that window."

They kept on until they were beneath the window.
Then they slowly raised themselves to their feet, and
looked in.

CHAPTER VII

A new life

"MR. SANFORD!"

Ellen was surprised to see the farmer. John just stood looking in for a moment, without saying a word. Hortense was out of her stall, in the part of the barn just inside the door. She seemed very restless, Ellen thought. Cows are always so calm. They stand still, or lie down, for hours without moving. But Hortense was restless.

"Oh, it's Hortense!" whispered John.

"What do you mean?" Ellen whispered back. "What is your father doing?"

"It's Hortense. She's calving. I wonder if Pa needs help. Ellen, you'd better go back to bed. I'll stay here and help Pa."

Champ had been lying in a corner of the barn. He heard their voices and raised his ears. Then he got up and came over to the window.

Mr. Sanford looked sharply toward the window. Quickly he crossed the floor and threw up the sash. "What are you children doing?" he demanded.

"We—we are—" Ellen began.

"We heard a noise and saw a light in the barn," John

explained. "We thought it might be burglars. We came out to see."

"There are no burglars. Go back to bed," ordered Mr. Sanford. "You children shouldn't be up this time of night. You ought to be in your beds, asleep."

"Yes, Mr. Sanford," said Ellen.

"Need any help, Pa?" asked John.

"No, son, I don't think so. You go back to bed and get your rest."

Ellen looked from John to Mr. Sanford. Back in the city things like this never happened. The farmer saw how puzzled she looked, and explained, "It's Hortense. Her calf is going to be born tonight."

"Her calf?" Now Ellen understood and she became very excited. "A little baby calf? Tonight? Oh, may I stay and wait for it to be born? May I, please?"

"No, Ellen, you'd better go back to the house. Your folks don't want you out of bed this late at night."

"I'll go ask them. If they say it's all right, then may I?" Ellen begged.

"What? Wake them up at this hour?"

"I don't think they'd mind. Anyway, I could try."

"But cows don't like people around when they're having a calf. Especially strangers," said Mr. Sanford.

"Strangers?" repeated Ellen. "Hortense let me pet her, didn't she? We're friends, not strangers."

Ellen's face had so brightened at the thought of seeing the baby calf that Mr. Sanford found it too hard to refuse. But he replied, "Ellen, I can't let you come out here to watch unless your parents say it's all right.

Especially at this hour, when you should be asleep."

"I'll go ask them!" Ellen was away like a flash, running through the darkness to the house. She raced upstairs, and knocked on the door.

"Mother! Daddy!"

"What's the matter?" came Dad's sleepy voice from inside the room.

"May I come in?"

"Yes. Come in. What is it? Fire?"

Ellen opened the door and ran over to Daddy.

"Hortense is in the barn, and . . ."

"Hortense?" Dad mumbled sleepily. "Who's Hortense?"

"Hortense is almost a cow, Daddy, and . . ."

"Who's almost a cow? Ellen, what are you talking about? I must be dreaming."

Ellen pinched Daddy. "There!" she said. "You're not dreaming."

Dad jumped out of bed, rubbing his pinch. "Now what is all this?" he shouted.

Mother was awake now and she said, "Ellen, what is it?"

"A calf, Mother! A baby calf!"

Mother sat up. Her eyes popped open. "Where?" she cried.

"Oh, Mother," said Ellen, "It's not here yet, but it's going to be. Tonight! Mr. Sanford said so. And he said we can see it be born. Hurry, please! Get up!"

"It would be a good thing for Ellen to see," Mother said to Dad, "I want her to learn about birth. Come on,

Dad, let's get dressed and go with Ellen."

"I'll go back to the barn awhile." Ellen bounded into the hall. Another door opened. Mrs. Sanford looked out.

"Good Heavens!" she exclaimed. "What's going on here?"

"Hortense is turning into a cow, and we're all going to watch her," Ellen shouted as she ran down the steps, two at a time.

She ran back to the barn. As she went in, she noticed some water on the floor. She asked Mr. Sanford about it.

He explained, "The baby calf grows in a bag inside its mother, in a place called the womb. The bag is filled with liquid. When it's ready to be born, the bag breaks and the liquid comes out. After that, the calf comes out very soon."

"Oh," said Ellen. "But how will it get out?"

"When it's ready to be born, muscles in Hortense's womb push it toward the birth passage and just keep on pushing until it comes out."

"Where's the birth passage?" asked Ellen.

"It's an opening above her udder and underneath her tail. It's called the vagina and it isn't used for anything except having baby calves. It leads from the womb where the baby calf grew and it stretches big enough to let the calf out. After the calf is born the vagina gets small again."

The voices and footsteps of Mr. and Mrs. Gordon and Mrs. Sanford could be heard nearing the barn.

Hortense was lying on the clean straw that Mr. Sanford ·
had spread for her. Her sides seemed to be moving in
and out.

"Her calf will be born any minute now," said Mrs.
Sanford. "It is moving toward the vagina."

In several minutes two clean little hoofs could be
seen under Hortense's tail. A moment later the little
calf's head started to show.

John and Ellen watched with interest. "Oh, it isn't
furry, is it?" Ellen said.

"Not furry?" John laughed. "Sure it is! It's still wet
from the liquid. Just you wait, Ellen, till it's dry and
fluffed up if you want to see something nice and furry."

The baby calf's front legs and head and neck were
out now. It opened its mouth and gasped for air.

"There, it got its breath," remarked Dad.

The rest of the calf came out. It lay on the fresh
straw with its little legs folded under it. A long, shiny
red cord went from the calf's belly into Hortense's
vagina. The calf was breathing as it should.

"How did it breathe before, in Hortense?" inquired
Ellen.

"Through this cord," answered Mr. Sanford. "The
calf got all its food and air, everything it needed,
through this cord."

"How?"

"The cord is connected to the baby calf here on its
belly." Mr. Sanford turned the calf to show her. "The
other end is connected to the inside of the bag that the
calf grew in. Blood vessels go through the cord to carry

the food and air from the mother to the baby."

After awhile, the cord started moving farther out of Hortense. Then the bag came out, still attached to the cord.

"Now the birth is over," said Dad. "The baby calf is on its own, now."

"Is that the bag the calf lived in?"

"Yes," said Mr. Sanford, "it was around the calf, filled with liquid, and it lined the inside of Hortense's womb."

"Oh, said Ellen, "the bag soaked up food from the mother and sent it through the cord to the baby calf?"

"That's right," answered the farmer. "You're a smart girl, Ellen."

Hortense was licking her baby calf with warm, loving strokes. It was drying, and beginning to look very soft and furry.

The farmer bent over the little calf. "We'll leave a few inches of the cord and cut the rest away," he said. "And now we'll put some iodine on it so germs won't infect it. In a few days this will dry up and drop off. The place where it was attached to the calf is called the navel."

Hortense was still contentedly licking her baby calf. Ellen watched, thrilled by the wonder of life that had brought this little creature into the world. She knelt down and touched its soft, velvety ears. She noticed its long black eyelashes, its big brown eyes. "Only this afternoon," she said, "I put my hand on Hortense's side and felt it moving. And now it's here." She patted it gently. "And now Hortense will have milk for her little calf and some left over for Mr. Sanford—I mean, for his milking machine. And maybe, after it's put in bottles, I'll be drinking some of it too."

Mr. and Mrs. Gordon and Mrs. Sanford and John had been looking on silently. But now Mr. Gordon spoke.

"That's right, Ellen. But it's all over now. I think you ought to go to bed. You can see the baby calf again in the morning."

"You, too, John," said Mrs. Sanford.

CHAPTER VIII

Going fishing

"COCK-A-DOODLE-DO-O-O-O!"

When the rooster awakened Ellen, she knew, as soon as she opened her eyes, that other people in the house were already up. She could hear Mrs. Sanford with the dishes in the kitchen. She heard John call something to his father in the barn. In the far distance, a church bell rang.

"Sunday!" Ellen told herself.

Then her mind went back to the night before. "The little baby calf! I must go out to see it!"

She jumped out of bed and in a few minutes she was downstairs, dressed, washed and combed, and tooth-brushed.

Mother was helping Mrs. Sanford in the kitchen. Ellen raced right through. "I have to see the baby calf," she explained as she ran.

"Ellen!" called Mrs. Gordon. "Ellen, you come back here!"

Ellen slid to a stop in the yard. "What is it, Mother?" she called back.

"Don't you run off now," said Mother. "You shouldn't have dressed in those slacks. Today is Sunday and we're all going to church together. You should have put on your pink dress."

"I'll be back in a minute, Mother."

"Mind you do. Breakfast is almost on the table."

Ellen skipped to the barn. The cows had already been let out to pasture. But Hortense was there with her baby calf. It was standing with its mother, its mouth on one of the nipples of her udder. The calf looked very cute and soft with its light-colored fur.

"Getting your breakfast?" Ellen asked. The calf didn't even notice Ellen. It just kept right on getting its breakfast.

"You have milk now, haven't you, Hortense?"

Hortense didn't even turn her head, but kept right on giving milk to her little calf.

John came in. He grinned. "You like that little calf, don't you, Ellen?" He reached over and petted it. "And you thought it wouldn't be nice and furry," he laughed.

"You were right," said Ellen. "But I never saw a calf born before."

"Well, if you'd been brought up on a farm, you would have. I've seen lots of animals born around here," said John. "But let's go back to the house, Ellen. Ma said breakfast is ready."

After breakfast, they all started for church. The Sanfords led the way in their car, and the Gordons followed in theirs. Mrs. Gordon and Ellen sat together on the back seat while Mr. Gordon drove.

They rode for awhile in silence past other farms. Then Ellen spoke. "Mother, how long did I grow inside you before I was born?"

"Nine months," answered Mother. "And when you were born you were the cutest baby there ever was. Cuter than a baby calf, or a kitten—even cuter than a chick."

"Oh, Mother," Ellen giggled.

"Well, anyway, I thought so."

"Was a cord attached to me when I was born?"

"Yes, dear. While you were inside me you grew in a bag filled with liquid, and food went to you through a cord connected to the inside of the bag. You know where your navel is?"

"Yes, right here," Ellen pointed.

"Well, that is where the cord was attached to you. When you were about a week old, it dried up and fell off."

"You were an awfully cute baby, Ellen," Dad joined in from the front seat. "I can see your mother yet, holding you in her arms, while you nursed at her breast."

Ellen said, "After I was born I drank milk from you, didn't I, Mother?"

"Yes, until you were weaned. Then you drank cow's milk from a little cup, and later you ate other foods."

"Well, here's the church," said Dad. "Mr. Sanford has stopped. I can park right in back of him."

The two families entered the old white church together. Ellen liked being in church. It always gave her a happy, contented feeling.

And then back to the Sanfords' for a dinner of delicious fried chicken. Ellen helped with the dishes.

Sunday afternoon was very quiet on the farm.

Monday was Memorial Day. Mr. Sanford said he couldn't leave his farm that morning. Mr. Gordon drove Ellen and John and Mother over to Newton to see the parade. After it was over, Dad drove them back to the farm.

After lunch, John got together the fishing poles and cans of bait. Ellen and John changed to their slacks and soon they were ready.

"Ellen," said Mother, "you'd better wear your sweater. It seems a little cool today."

Ellen put on her sweater, and then she and John were on their way, with Champ trotting beside them.

They passed a field with a heavy fence around it. There was only one animal in it. Ellen wondered why that one cow should be separated from the others, why it had a metal ring in its nose, and why it kept butting the fence with its head. It seemed larger than the other cows, too. She would have asked John about it, but she had already asked so many questions. Besides, he was telling her all about fish right now. It didn't seem just right to ask a question about cows when he was talking about fish.

Soon they were by the stream. Ellen could hear its wonderful music—the gay bubbling sounds of the quick water as it laughed its way over the rocks. The warm spring sunshine went right through Ellen's sweater. She took it off and hung it on a branch. Then she stood quietly looking at the wide stream. It wound its way as far as she could see. Willow trees hung over its banks, and above it the sky shone clear and blue.

"It's prettier than any painted picture I ever saw," she said to John.

"I think so, too," he agreed, as he baited the hooks.

They sat down on the bank of the stream. After some time, Ellen nudged John with her elbow and pointed to her fishline. It was trembling.

"You've got a bite!" John whispered. "Hook it! Flip your pole up a little. You've got it! Pull it in! Easy, don't break your line."

CHAPTER IX

Ellen's danger

ELLEN BEGAN WINDING up her line. This was the first time she had gone fishing and she was very excited.

"Oo-oo, John," she exclaimed as she saw a beautiful fish struggling on the end of her line.

"Say, that's a beauty. You're really good, Ellen."

"Oh, I guess it's just beginner's luck," said Ellen, as John unhooked the fish.

"I can bait my own hook this time," she boasted, picking up a worm. "Ugh!"

"Good for you!" smiled John.

And into the stream again went Ellen's line. Then quiet and stillness. And again the delight of feeling a fish nibble the bait.

But just then, John nudged Ellen. "I've got one," he whispered.

"Me, too!" Ellen whispered back.

They pulled in together, and two struggling fish appeared above the stream.

"Yours is bigger than mine," Ellen shouted.

"It sure is," John laughed, taking the hook out of the big fish's mouth.

Ellen had put her fish away, and was baiting her hook again.

"I'm going to catch dozens and dozens just as I said," she declared, casting her line again.

But by the time they were ready to return to the farmhouse, John had caught many more than Ellen.

They walked along the stream by the weeping willow trees. Ellen was watching the leaf shadows play on the water when suddenly a frog leaped across her path.

"Catch him!" shouted Ellen, leaping after him.

"I'll get him!" cried John, scrambling down the bank. He jumped into the middle of a clump of plants growing by the edge of the water. He came up with a kicking, frightened frog in his hands.

"Here he is. Are you going to take him home with you?"

"To my home? Oh, no. I'll just show him to Mother and Daddy and then I'll let him go."

John placed the slippery frog in Ellen's hands with a warning. "Don't put your hand under his feet. If you do, he'll kick against your hand and slip away. Swish! and he'll be gone. Hold him around his middle."

They walked away from the stream, toward the farmhouse. They passed the field that had the one cow with the ring in the end of its nose. It was quietly grazing.

"Oh!" said Ellen suddenly. "My sweater! I haven't got it!"

"You hung it on a branch," John recalled.

"I know. I forgot to bring it with me. We have to go back for it."

"I'll get it," John offered. "You stay right here. I'll be right back."

He was off, running back to the brook with Champ at his heels. Ellen looked at the frog she was holding. It was dark green, shiny and slippery, with dark brown spots. It had round, blinking eyes, and long, webbed feet on its folded legs. Ellen wanted to get a good look at its funny little face. Forgetting John's warning, she cupped her hand under it. This was just what those two strong legs had been waiting for. They sprang out suddenly, with a hard kick against her hand. Swish! The slippery body shot forth as if it had been greased. With a smooth dive, it landed on the ground.

Ellen gasped and swooped down to catch it. But it leaped away. Every time she got near it, it leaped. It seemed to be heading for a pile of hay that stood near the fence. A long-handled pitchfork was stuck in the hay.

"If it gets into that," thought Ellen, "I'll never get it. It'll be like looking for a leaping needle in a haystack."

With a quick jump, she got between the frog and the haystack. The frog turned and leaped through the fence.

"It's getting away!"

Ellen ran to the fence and scrambled over it. When she looked for her frog, it was nowhere to be seen.

"It's gone!" she cried.

Suddenly she heard a loud, angry snort. She looked up. The animal with the ring in its nose was glaring at her. Ellen watched it with fright as it lowered its head and started toward her. There was no time to climb back over the fence to safety. There was only time to run. As fast as she could, she ran beside the fence, her heart pounding.

The big animal started after her. It was getting closer to her, kicking up a cloud of dust and snorting loudly. Ellen was coming to a corner of the fence. Half blind with fear, she turned the corner. The animal swung, too, cutting the corner, and getting even closer to her! She must not turn corners! The beast would overtake her! Better to run in a circle!

The thud of his hoofs grew louder and louder. She didn't know which way to run. There was no place to escape. Her legs were becoming stiff with fear. She couldn't keep on much longer. She tried to scream for help, but she could only gasp and keep on running. Her legs seemed no longer to belong to her. She was running blindly and praying for someone to save her before it was too late.

CHAPTER X

The rescue

"Ellen! ellen!"

It was John's voice. Ellen saw him, as through a mist, climbing over the fence. What was he holding? The long pitchfork that she had seen stuck in that pile of hay. Here was help at last! She took a deep breath and tried to keep on running. If only she could hold out!

Something else streaked across the fence and dashed ahead of John. A brown and white streak! Champ! It was Champ!

The big collie dog ran at the huge beast. His loud barking drowned out the noise of the thundering hoofs and angry snorting. It shied away, its hoofs skidding on the ground in a cloud of dust. With a wild snort, the brute turned to charge at Champ. But as it did so, it turned its face toward the sharp tines of the pitchfork. For John had arrived with surprising speed. He prayed that his arms and legs would stop trembling long enough to slip the fork into the ring in the animal's nose, and that Ellen would have sense enough to climb over the fence. As the beast snorted and charged toward him, he quickly pushed the pitchfork into the ring—

and it held! The animal had to back away as John breathlessly pushed the fork against the ring. Champ was running circles around the beast, barking loudly. John pushed on. From the corner of his eye he saw that Ellen was over the fence. She was safe!

John forced the animal to the other side of the field. Attached to the fence was a strong iron chain with a clamp on one end. Holding the pitchfork with one hand, he grabbed the chain with the other. Then, with one quick movement, he hooked the clamp into the ring on the end of the beast's nose. Ellen watched as John turned and ran. The animal started after him, but was stopped short by the chain. John leaped over the fence to safety on the other side. At last! It was over!

"What did you go in the bull's pen for?" John asked angrily, his voice still shaking.

"Bull?" questioned Ellen. "That cow's not a bull, is it?"

"That bull is a bull," replied John. "Humph! It's easy to tell you're a city girl. That's Horace. But why did you go in there?"

"My frog. It got away. It hopped in there, and I went after it."

"You went after trouble when you went in there," said John, wiping his face on the back of his arm. "You're lucky you're alive. He could have killed you."

Ellen looked up at John, her eyes filling with tears. "You're so brave. Just like a bullfighter. How can I ever thank you for saving my life?"

"Forget it," John said. Then he leaned over and gave

Champ a hard pat. "Thank him! If it hadn't been for my dog I couldn't have saved you."

Ellen put her arm around the collie. "Good old Champ," she whispered.

"Let's get our things and go home," said John.

Soon they were back at the farmhouse.

"Why, Ellen!" exclaimed Mrs. Sanford. "You're pale —and you're trembling! What's the matter? What happened to you?"

"She got into the bull pen and Horace chased her," declared John. "He nearly caught her, too."

"And John saved me," added Ellen.

They told Mrs. Sanford the whole story. She put her arm around Ellen. "You poor little girl. How frightened you must have been. You sit right here while I fix some hot tea."

Mrs. Sanford looked with pride at her son, saying quietly, "I'm glad you're so brave, John." Then she began to prepare tea.

John noticed that his mother's eyes had tears in them, just as Ellen's had when she thanked him. "Gee," he thought, "men don't cry over nothing, like that." Still, he whistled happily as he put the fish in the sink. Then he left the room to put away the fishing tackle. In a few minutes he returned.

"I don't like that nasty old bull," Ellen told Mrs. Sanford over a cup of hot tea.

"No, I guess you don't, Ellen."

Ellen continued, "He doesn't give milk or anything, does he?"

John laughed out loud. "Who ever heard of anyone milking a bull?"

"Well, then, what good is he?" asked Ellen. "He isn't cute at all, and even if he were, he's too big to be a pet. He has no milk—he must eat a dreadful lot—why do you keep him?"

"Now you stop talking against Horace," Mrs. Sanford shook her finger at Ellen.

"But, why does he have to be so mean? Chasing me! I wasn't going to hurt him! My frog wasn't going to hurt him!"

"He isn't really mean, Ellen. It's just a bull's way, that's all."

"Well, gee, why did he chase me?" asked Ellen.

Mrs. Sanford looked very thoughtful, as if she were trying to think of an answer.

Then John said, "Maybe Pa can tell us. . . . Pa!"

"Yes, John?" called Mr. Sanford from the next room.

"Ellen wants to know—what makes bulls so mean?"

"Well," declared the farmer, walking into the kitchen with his newspaper in his hand. He rubbed his chin, saying slowly to himself, "Why did Horace chase Ellen? Let's see now, if I can explain it to you, Ellen."

He sat down and began, "I guess there was a time, long, long ago, when all cattle were wild. That was before people started keeping them in fields with fences around them. Cattle were on their own then. And there must have been plenty of hungry wolves and animals like that around, just waiting for a chance to go after a poor little calf or its mother cow." Mr. Sanford took out his handkerchief and began polishing his eyeglasses.

"Gosh!" said Ellen. "Who protected them?"

"Well, now," said Mr. Sanford, "that's just where the bulls come in, Ellen. The bulls had to take care of the cows and calves. Every time they saw anything strange coming around, they'd charge at 'em and scare 'em away. And they got so used to doing this, it became a habit with them—a habit they never got rid of—even to this day." Mr. Sanford stood up. "There now, I've explained it as best I could. I'm going back and finish reading my paper."

"Golly," said Ellen. "It's a good thing bulls were like that or I guess people wouldn't have any cows today at all."

"Nope," agreed John. "We'd probably all be drinking nannygoat milk."

Ellen laughed. Mrs. Sanford said, "Well, everything's all right now, isn't it, Ellen? You're not mad at Horace any more?"

"Oh, no," said Ellen. "It just seems funny to me now. But there's one thing I'll never forget—how John protected me. He was wonderful."

CHAPTER XI

An invitation

THE OUTSIDE KITCHEN DOOR opened. Mr. and Mrs. Gordon entered.

"Oh, Mommy, Daddy, where have you been?" cried Ellen as she ran and threw her arms about her mother. "I was nearly killed by a bull and John and Champ rescued me. And John nearly got killed, too."

"What's all this?" asked Dad, as Ellen turned to him. He sat down and drew her to him and she told him all that had happened.

When she finished Dad stood up and held out his hand. "John, how can I ever thank you for saving Ellen's life?" He gripped the boy's hand.

John felt uncomfortable. Why was everyone so serious? "It was nothing," he said in a voice that seemed rude, even to himself.

"Nothing, is it?" said Dad. "To risk your life to save Ellen?"

Mother came over to John. Her eyes were wet and Ellen knew that Mother was almost ready to cry as she thanked him.

Then Dad said it was now time for them to get packed

up for home, but first they had an important question to settle. When could the Sanfords come to visit them in the city? Ellen and John danced around shouting, "Oh, boy! Oh, boy! When? When?"

Mr. and Mrs. Sanford thanked Dad, but explained there never could be a recess for the whole family from farm work. Mr. Sanford started to name all the jobs of farming which they couldn't leave, until Dad shouted, "Stop it! You're making me feel like a lazy loafer."

Mr. Sanford laughed. "Why, farming is not so hard nowadays, what with all the machinery and everything to help us. All the same, we can't leave the farm. But John could visit you without us, maybe during summer vacation from school."

Ellen and John looked at each other. Their faces lit up and they started to grin. "Oh, Boy!" they shouted together.

The parents laughed and everything was settled.

Later that evening, after everything was packed and put in the car, the Gordons and the Sanfords said their last good-byes. Champ was hugged a farewell, Ellen took a last look at Hortense and her little calf, and she patted Sophie and Dignity and gave them some sugar cubes. She waved good-bye to Horace, too, for now that she understood him, all was forgiven.

And then they were off for home, leaving the peaceful, quiet farm. They rode along the smooth highway, heading back to towns and cities where life was quick again.

"It's like coming out of church into a busy street,"

Ellen remarked to Mother. "Coming from the nice, peaceful farm to the hurry-up things again."

"Are you sorry to leave the farm?" asked Dad.

"Yes, I had so much fun there," said Ellen. "And wasn't John brave the way he protected me?"

"I'm glad we saw Hortense's little calf born, too," said Mother.

"Is Horace the little calf's father?" asked Ellen.

"Yes, that's why farmers keep a bull," answered Dad. "For the same reason they keep roosters. Before a calf can start to grow, the bull has to fertilize a tiny, one-cell egg in the body of the cow."

"Oh, the cow's egg is smaller than a hen's egg?"

"So small you can hardly see it. The hen's egg is large because the chick grows outside the mother's body. The egg has to hold all the food for the growing chick. A calf grows inside the mother. It gets its food from the mother as it grows."

"Does Horace have sperm cells, too?" asked Ellen.

"Yes," answered Mother. "They grow in his testicles."

"What are they?"

"Well, you know where the cow has her udder?"

"Yes."

"The bull, of course, has no udder, but at that same place on a bull, there's a sort of little bag. Inside it are two oval-shaped testicles. Tiny sperm cells, millions of them, grow inside."

"Oh, I know what you mean, Mother," said Ellen. "Brownie has that and in front of it he has a little thing like a tube."

"That little tube is his penis," said Mother. "He has that because he's a male dog."

"But how do the bull's sperm cells get to the egg cell in the mother cow?" asked Ellen.

"Well, you remember where the baby calf came out of Hortense?"

"Yes. The vagina."

"That's right. It leads to the womb where the baby calf has to grow. And that's where the sperm cells have to enter to fertilize the egg cell."

"Well," Ellen asked, "how do the sperm cells get into the vagina?"

"They go in through the penis, which fits into it," Mother replied.

"Oh, is that like the little tube that Brownie has?"

"Yes, just the same. Remember what I told you about the rooster, Ellen?" Daddy asked. "How his sperm cells swim in a liquid called semen?"

"Yes, I remember," said Ellen. "You said they were so tiny you'd have to use a microscope to see them."

"That's right. Well, the bull has semen, too, with sperm cells in it. When the semen is left inside the cow, they start swimming to the egg cell."

"How can they swim?" asked Ellen.

"Each one has a quick little tail," answered Dad. "They swim by wriggling their tails back and forth very fast. With a microscope you'd see that."

"And when they find the egg cell, do they all try to get in?" asked Ellen.

"Yes, but just as soon as one gets in, the egg is fertilized. Then no other sperm cell can get in. The life of the baby calf has now begun, and the egg cell divides in half, making two cells. Those two divide again, making four, and so on, until millions of cells form together to make a complete calf."

"Yes, even to its eyelashes, and fuzzy little ears," added Mother. "And when everything's finished and perfect, the little calf comes out of its mother and into the world."

"I never knew all that before," said Ellen. "And is it the same way with people, too?"

"Of course. Mothers have little eggs that you can hardly see, and fathers have sperm cells. That's what makes men different from women."

"Oh," said Ellen. "And the father has to put his cells inside the mother to start a little baby growing?"

"Yes, after people get married and want a baby."

"I grew from a tiny little egg cell, didn't I?" Ellen stretched her arms and legs as far as she could on the back seat of the car, and smiled. "But just look at me now!"

Dad and Mother laughed. Ellen looked out of the car window. A red-gold sun was setting in back of purple hills, and a soft breeze was blowing back her hair as they drove along. Suddenly she felt how good it was to be alive.

"Gee, I'm glad you and Mommy got married and wanted me, or I wouldn't even be here," she said. "And won't it feel good to get home?"

"Yes. I wonder what Fred's doing now," said Mother.

"Probably out with Nancy," answered Dad. "You see, Ellen, before people get married they go together for some time to make sure they really love each other and are happy together. After they get married they should stay together all their lives."

"I see." Ellen pictured Fred out with Nancy, and her little dog home all alone. She sat up. "Brownie! I wonder what Brownie's doing now?"

"Probably eating pieces out of my best house slippers," Dad remarked.

"Oh, dear, I hope not," Ellen cried. "It might hurt him. Please drive faster, Daddy. I want to get home to my Brownie."

"And I want to get home to my slippers!"

CHAPTER XII

Ellen becomes a partner

A<small>T THAT VERY MOMENT</small>, in the living room of the Gordon home, Brownie was having a wonderful time playing cat and mouse with one of Dad's best slippers. Fred was sitting in an easy chair, studying. The telephone rang. He reached for it.

"Hello." Then his face lit up as if a light had been turned on inside him. "Oh, hello Nancy. . . . No, just studying. What are you doing?"

Just then Brownie began to bark. He caught up Dad's slipper in his mouth and ran to the front door with it.

"Do you hear Brownie?" Fred spoke into the telephone. "He heard the car in the drive. The family's arriving home and he's all excited. Have to say good-bye now, but don't forget—dinner tomorrow night at that little restaurant you like. 'Bye, Nancy."

As he hung up, Brownie was being greeted by Ellen who had bounded in at the front door.

"Brownie!" she scolded, grabbing Dad's slipper from his mouth. The naughty puppy sat up, looked very bright, and wagged his tail. Thump! Thump! It beat the floor.

"Oh, Brownie, you shouldn't have done it," Ellen cried, looking at the shapeless slipper. It had been tossed about, bitten and chewed, till it looked like anything but something to fit a man's foot.

Dad followed Ellen into the living room, yelling, "Where are my slippers? Where's that pup?"

Ellen held the slipper behind her back and faced her father. Brownie got in back of Ellen and peeked through her legs.

"Ah," cried Dad, pointing. "There he is!"

Brownie wagged his tail and looked guilty.

Ellen brought the slipper forth. "He didn't bite any pieces out of it, Daddy." She held it up. "See? Not even one little piece."

Dad took the slipper. "Oh, my gosh!" he said. "I can't tell the toe from the heel any more. I don't happen to have a round foot, you know." He threw the slipper across the room. Brownie dashed after it and brought it back to Dad, merrily wagging his tail.

Dad looked down at the little dog. He pursed his lips to keep the smile in. "You ought to be ashamed of yourself, Brownie, chewing on a man's best slipper."

Ellen knelt down and hugged her pet. "Isn't he cute, Daddy?" Then they both petted him together while Brownie's tail beat the floor. He'd won again.

Fred had just greeted Mother and he called "Hi!" to Ellen and Dad.

"How was golf?" asked Dad. "Did you make a hole in one?"

"No, but Nancy almost did. What a girl!"

"No girl like Nancy, eh?" Dad smiled.

"No girl in all the world like Nancy, Dad. I was just talking with her on the phone, and we made a date for dinner tomorrow night. May I borrow the car, Dad?"

"Yes, I don't suppose I'll be using it." He turned to Mother. "Isn't it cool in here? Shall I burn some logs in the fireplace?"

"Oh, splendid!" Mother answered.

Ellen loved this. "Let me help," she offered. "And I'm going to toast marshmallows, too."

"All right," said Dad. "Put the fire screen aside, and get your marshmallows."

Ellen obeyed. She came back with a box of marshmallows. Dad was stacking logs in the fireplace. "It's all ready to light," he said.

In a few minutes, bright flames were curling and dancing around the logs. Mother had been upstairs unpacking the bags. Now she came down, comfortable in her blue housecoat. At the foot of the stairs she switched off the living room light, saying, "Let's just have the light from the fire. The flames look so beautiful in the dark."

"Still the campfire girl?" Dad teased.

"Oh, yes!" Mother came over and kissed Dad's cheek. "Still love marshmallows, too," she said to Ellen.

Ellen laughed and stuck a plump marshmallow on the end of a toasting-stick and handed it to Mother. She took it and knelt in front of the fire. The flames put dancing lights on her face. She was laughing happily and she looked like a young girl again. "Mother's beautiful," thought Ellen, and judging from the way her father was looking at her mother, he thought so, too.

Dad and Fred sat down in the colonial wing chairs on each side of the fireplace. Father and son looked very much alike. They were both very tall with hair like black satin, but Dad's was turning silver. They both had velvety-brown eyes, but Dad had to wear glasses.

Fred sat looking dreamily into the fire for a minute or so. Then he began, "You know I want to marry Nancy, don't you, Dad?"

"Your mother told me."

"Nancy's the right girl for me, Dad," Fred said. "We're very well suited to each other. And we're interested in the same things."

"I know you are." Dad lit his pipe. "What with Nancy working to be an artist and you to be an architect, you both enjoy the same things. You'll have fun together all your lives."

Mother was listening and she added. "They both have

the same religion, too. There won't be any argument over which church to go to, when they have children."

"That's right, but most important of all . . ." Fred began.

"Yes, most important of all," said Dad, "you understand and love each other."

Ellen wasn't too busy toasting marshmallows to remark, "Nancy's awfully pretty, too."

"Beauty doesn't mean so very much," said Dad. "If a girl's just pretty on the outside, she may become quite plain as time goes on. But if her character is good and sweet it will show on her face, and she'll stay beautiful forever."

"Like Mother?" asked Ellen.

"Yes, like your mother." Dad took his pipe from his mouth and smiled at Mother. Then he spoke to Fred. "Marriage is a wonderful thing—a home of your own— children of your own. Why, without my wife, my children, and my home . . ."

"You'd be awfully lonely without us, wouldn't you, Daddy?" Ellen chewed a marshmallow with great satisfaction.

"You bet I would," replied Dad. "Although it isn't just marriage that keeps a man from being lonely. I know of some married people who took the wrong partner for life. And now they live alone because they are not loved, even though they are sharing a house with someone."

Dad's words made Mother very thoughtful. She was sitting on the floor, looking into the fire, watching it turn a plump white marshmallow golden brown. Then she spoke as if to herself. "All the years ahead, the young years, the middle-aged years, the old, quiet years, all to be spent with the one person you choose to eat, sleep, and live with in the same house. If there is any more important choice for young people to make, I'm sure I can't think what it could be."

"You and Mother are so happy together," said Fred. "And I know Nancy and I will be, too. Dad, I'd like to marry Nancy right after we graduate from college in June."

Dad's eyes and mouth popped open. "What's that? In June? Next month?"

"Oh, I know what you're going to say," Fred replied. You and Mother sent me to college to learn to be an architect. You don't want me to get married until I'm earning a living as an architect. But I could get another job for the time being. Nancy and I could get along somehow."

"And what if you and Nancy have children while you're in that 'time-being' job, just getting along?" asked Mother.

"Then the 'time-being' job may become the life-long rut!" Dad exclaimed. "No, my son, that isn't going to happen to you! I want you started in your work as an architect before you marry Nancy."

"But, Dad, I love Nancy so. I want to be with her all the time. I want the right to call her my wife."

"Then you must first earn that right." Dad took his pipe from his mouth and looked at Fred. "Life isn't a sugar-plum tree from which you can pick anything you want without working for it."

Fred sat thinking. The room was very silent but for the crackling of the logs in the fireplace. After awhile he looked up.

"I see what you mean, Dad. I guess I've been living in a sort of dream world lately."

"All young people in love do that," Daddy smiled. "But you don't have to give up your dreams. You just have to work very hard to bring them to life, that's all."

As Dad spoke, a smile began to spread over Fred's face.

"Dad, you've just given me an idea. 'Bring your dreams to life,' you said. Oh, boy, wait till I see Nancy tomorrow night. Wait'll I tell her what I'm planning to do!"

"Tell me! Tell me!" Ellen begged.

"I have to tell Nancy first," said Fred. "She has to help me."

"But I want to help, too."

"We won't go ahead with anything without first asking for your advice," Fred promised.

"Cross your heart?" asked Ellen. She wasn't sure, since Fred had winked at Dad.

"Cross my heart, and now say good night."

Mother laughed. "That's right. It's your bedtime, Ellen."

"Good night." Ellen reached up and hugged her tall brother. He bent down and she whispered sleepily in his ear. "It'll be fun bringing dreams to life, won't it? Tell Nancy I'm a partner, too."

CHAPTER XIII

The plans

F RED PARKED the family car in front of Nancy's house at seven o'clock, and rang the doorbell. He heard Nancy's footsteps hurrying to the door. Then her cheerful welcome, "Hi, Fred! I'm all ready."

Fred looked with pride at Nancy. "Hello, Beautiful!"

"Thank you," Nancy smiled as she and Fred walked into the living room. They chatted for awhile with Nancy's parents. Then they said good-bye as Fred held the front door open for Nancy. "Have a good time," called Mr. and Mrs. Clark.

Soon they were inside the neat, cozy restaurant, seated at a small table covered with snowy-white linen. After both orders had been given to the waitress, Fred looked at Nancy with shining eyes. "Nancy," he said, "while we're waiting to get married, this is what I plan to do." He started talking so fast Nancy could hardly catch all the words. But the ones that excited her most were "you help with the plans" "this will be our dream house" "you plan the kitchen and the nursery" and "what do you think of painting it white with red shutters and a red roof, and flower boxes?"

"Oh, Fred," said Nancy. "It will be the most wonderful house in all the world. We'll do it together."

"It'll be the best house ever built," Fred went on happily. "And it can be built for so low a price almost anybody could afford it. And another thing I almost forgot to tell you—I'm getting a job lined up with the firm of Brown and Morgan. I want to start working right after I graduate."

"Brown and Morgan?" exclaimed Nancy. "Why, that's the biggest firm of architects around here. Oh, Fred, you're wonderful."

"I called on Mr. Morgan yesterday," Fred said. "He told me to come in to see him right after I graduate. He said he'll see what he can do for me."

"Next week," said Nancy, "we'll be studying for exams. We won't get much time to work on the plans, will we? But the week after we can work hard on them."

"Oh, we'll finish the plans all right. I have to do my part first. I'll work on them every night till one or two in the morning if I have to."

"You mustn't work too hard, Fred."

"The man who never works hard never gets anywhere," Fred replied. "Besides, I want to get them done as soon as possible. It's going to be such a wonderful house—our house!"

A few weeks later, they both were graduated from college. Fred as an architect, and Nancy as an artist.

The following day, Fred got up early, put on his best suit, and took the bus downtown to the firm of Brown and Morgan. He returned home in the evening, looking very tired. He sat down, wearily.

"They didn't have a job for me," he told Dad. "I've been trying other places all day, but—no luck. I'd take any kind of a job just to be earning a living. Hang it all, Dad, a fellow likes to feel that he can at least support himself."

Dad thought for a minute. Then he asked, "How would you like to be a salesman? I had lunch with John Weber today. He's in the screen business, you know. He said he could use a good salesman. You get paid for what you sell. You could still look for work as an architect in your spare time."

Fred did take the job. One evening he came home, put his case of samples down on the living room floor and sank into a chair.

"Whew! I'm tired," he exclaimed. "Been on my feet all day, talking to one person after another and didn't make enough sales to make a living for myself."

Brownie sat on the floor between Fred's feet, just looking at him with bright eyes.

"Hello, Brownie, you lucky dog!" said Fred.

Ellen brought him a glass of chilled tomato juice. "Thanks, Sis, you're swell," he said.

Ellen wished with all her heart that she could help her big brother get started in his life's work. "But I'll think of something," she said to herself, "I know I will."

Just then Mother walked into the room. "This came for you this afternoon," she said to Ellen, handing her a letter.

Ellen looked at the return address. "Wow! It's from

John." She tore the letter open. "He says he'll be able to visit us the week after next. He's coming by train because his father's too busy to drive him down. We'll meet him at the station."

It was a hot July afternoon when John arrived. As soon as he stepped off the train he began to look over the crowd for the familiar faces of the Gordon family. There he stood, a sunburned boy of eleven, with light hair, gay blue eyes, and a clean country look about him. He had a suitcase in one hand and in the other, a box with holes punched in the sides. He stood waiting to be seen—waiting for Ellen's "Hi!"

"Arf!" "Hi!" came both at once to his ears as he saw Ellen rushing toward him with Brownie in her arms.

"Hi!" John greeted her.

"This is Brownie," said Ellen. John put down his suitcase and petted Brownie. Ellen and John's laughter bubbled over with the joy of seeing each other again. And then John saw Mr. and Mrs. Gordon coming through the crowd. As they drove home, John told Ellen that the baby calf had grown very big, that Dignity and Sophie were fine, that the roosters crowed as loudly as ever, and that there was something in the box for her.

"Peep, peep!" said the box.

John lifted the lid a crack. Ellen peeked in. Two chicks peeked out. Ellen laughed. "When we get home, will you help me fix a box for them?"

Mother spoke from the front seat of the car. "Suppose you and John do that while I prepare dinner. I've invited Nancy, too."

Having special guests for dinner always made the house as gay as a music box. It meant a very good dinner, too, with something especially good for dessert. Mother's best silver and prettiest dishes would be used, and Ellen would gather red roses from the garden. She would put them in a vase in the center of the table, and their redness would make the tablecloth and napkins seem whiter than snow.

Mother and Ellen had just finished setting the table. "It looks as pretty as a picture in a magazine," said Ellen. "It makes me feel hungry, too."

After dinner, Ellen put on a big apron to help Mother with the dishes, while John cleared the table. Fred and Nancy went into the living room together. Mother told Dad she'd be ready as soon as the dishes were done. She and Dad were going to a party that evening at a friend's house.

CHAPTER XIV

The secret plot

"ALL FINISHED!" said Ellen as she handed John the big apron to hang away on the hook she couldn't reach. "Let's go in the living room."

They sat down together and John picked up one of Fred's old magazines.

"What are you reading that old thing for?" asked Ellen. "Gee, Fred bought that a long time ago."

"It sure has a nice picture of a ranch house on the cover," said John. "Dad hopes to build us a ranch house some day."

Fred and Nancy were sitting facing each other by the fireplace. Nancy was smiling at Fred.

"Guess what!" she said.

"What?" Fred smiled.

"I have a job!"

Fred unsmiled. "You have?"

"Yes. In an art agency. I start Monday. I'm going to make drawings for ads in newspapers."

"That's great," said Fred. "You can go out and get a job right away, doing the kind of work you like. But I have to sell screens. Humph!"

Mother and Dad came down from upstairs. They said good night to Nancy, Fred, Ellen and John. Everyone wished them a pleasant evening, and they left.

"Maybe with your salary and mine together. . . ." Nancy began.

"No, Nancy," Fred spoke slowly. "It would be a long time before we'd have enough money saved for a down payment on our house. And nobody would give me a loan unless I were earning money every week to pay it back. And we'd have to buy furniture, too. We couldn't live in an empty house."

"But, I'd be happy just to be with you, no matter where it was," said Nancy. "We could get married and live in a couple of rooms, if that's all we can afford."

"Would you, Nancy? But you wanted a home of your own, didn't you?"

"Yes, of course," replied Nancy. "But . . ."

"Well, then," said Fred. "you're going to have it. I have to be earning enough money before we get married. We can't plan on putting our two salaries together, either, because as soon as we have a baby you'll have to stay home. You'll have to give up your job to take care of the baby."

"Indeed I shall," declared Nancy. "No one but Nancy Clark herself is going to take care of our baby."

"Who?" grinned Fred.

"Mrs. Fred Gordon," corrected Nancy, laughing.

"That's better. And I have to have a good home ready for it."

"Listen, Fred," said Nancy, suddenly. "Why can't we

build a much cheaper house? We don't have to have our dream house. Something cheaper will do. And we could have it ready sooner."

Fred thought a minute.

"I think I could design a house that would cost only half as much, but it would have to be much smaller." He got up from his chair, opened the drawer of a large desk and took out a roll of papers. He returned to his chair, removed some rubber bands and unrolled some drawings—the drawings on which he had worked so hard.

"Maybe," said Nancy, "with just a few changes on these plans, we could. . . ."

"No," said Fred, studying the drawings carefully. "We can't use these drawings at all. The whole house would have to be smaller from the cellar up. Everything all through the house has to be cheaper. We'll just have to make a new set of plans."

Nancy stood up. "Well, there's no time like the present. We may as well begin right now."

"All right." Fred rolled up the drawings and put back the rubber bands. Then he went to the coat closet, opened it, and threw the roll of drawings on the top shelf.

"Let's work at the dining room table," he said to Nancy.

They left the room. Ellen and John were still sitting together with the magazine in front of them. But they weren't reading it. They were talking together in low voices.

"Now stop worrying about whether it's going to work," John was saying. "Just leave everything to me and it'll work all right."

"If it does—WOW!" said Ellen, all excited. "It'll be wonderful! Only . . ."

"What?" asked John. "What are you worrying about now?"

"I don't know," Ellen whispered. "Gee, we're taking such an awful chance, that's all."

"Gee whiz, you're not going to back out, are you?"

"No!" Ellen declared. "I promised, and I never break a promise."

"Good!" said John. "But I still think you'd feel better about it, if you'd ask him first."

"No, no, I can't. It would spoil everything. Because I know he wouldn't let us."

"Well, how do you know he wouldn't, till you ask?"

"Because he's my own brother, isn't he? And I guess I know my own brother, don't I? He wouldn't let us, and anyway, I don't want to ask him."

"Okay! Then we go ahead without asking!" John decided. "But not right now. Better come down in the middle of the night when everybody's asleep."

"Oh, no, John. We'd have to turn on the light and Brownie would bark and wake everybody up. We'd be caught and everything would be spoiled. Tomorrow in the daytime would be better. Dad and Fred will be out at work and Mother will be too busy to pay any attention to us, I know."

The following morning they were back in the living

room. Mother was icing a chocolate cake in the kitchen and singing softly.

"Now's our chance," whispered John. "I have the wrapping paper." He lifted the cushion of an overstuffed chair and showed Ellen a folded piece of brown paper. "I'll have to stand on a chair to reach them." He took the chair from beside the desk and carried it to the coat closet.

"Careful!" Ellen whispered as the chair knocked.

"Don't make me nervous," said John.

"No, I won't, but hurry!" she whispered. "Mother might come in any minute, so hurry!"

Mother could be heard humming as she iced the cake in the kitchen. John stepped up on the chair and snatched the roll of drawings from the shelf. Quickly, he stepped down and hid them behind an overstuffed chair near the door, closed the closet and put back the chair.

"That's fine!" Ellen whispered. Then she called, "Mother! . . . John and I are going out to play with the kids."

"All right, dear," Mother called back. "Be home in time for lunch."

"We will," promised Ellen. They snatched up the roll of drawings and the brown paper and ran out of the house. When they were half a block away, John said, "I'll take them. You stay here and wait for me. Here come Alice and Pat. Play with them till I get back."

Ellen agreed. John put the drawings and brown paper under his arm and walked quickly down the street.

In a little while he returned.

"Did you do it?" asked Ellen.

"It's all done," John told her with a quick grin.

Ellen sighed. "Thank Goodness!"

At the end of the week, John went back to the farm. Ellen promised to let him know how everything turned out.

What is all this mystery? What have Ellen and John done? Will their act be found out? Will they be punished?

CHAPTER XV

The missing papers

"HI, FOLKS! Wait'll you hear this!"
Fred burst through the front door, and threw his sample case down in the middle of the living room floor, shook the snow from his coat and hat and shouted, "Hey, where is everybody?"

"What is it?" Mother ran in from the kitchen.

"What's the matter?" Ellen ran down from upstairs.

"Arf?" Brownie ran up from the cellar.

"I'm going to get a job as an architect!" Fred exclaimed. "I called at a house today and a man came to the door. I gave him my sales talk. Then he looked surprised and asked how I knew he was building all those houses. Well, I didn't know what houses he was talking about. Anyway, I laughed and said, 'Oh, I sort of get around.' Then he said, 'Boy, you sure do! Why, I've just bought that land. I haven't even hired an architect yet.' Then I told him I could get him a good architect named Fred Gordon. Then he said, 'Never heard of him. Who's he?'"

Mother laughed. "What did you say then?"

"I don't remember exactly. But that man turned out

91

to be Mr. Luse, the president of the Luse Construction Company. They've just bought all that vacant land out in the Oakdale section, and they're planning to build a hundred and sixty one-family houses on it."

"Is he going to give you the job?"

"I don't know. He asked me where I worked before and I had to tell him I graduated from college only last June. He needs just one set of plans, because all the houses are going to be built very much alike. But it would give me a start and help me get a job somewhere else when this is done."

"That'll be wonderful," said Mother, as Fred hung up his coat in the hall closet.

"You remember the first set of plans Nancy and I worked on? Well, I told Mr. Luse he could use those plans just as they are and save himself a great deal of time."

"Do you suppose he would?" asked Mother.

"I don't see any reason why he shouldn't. They're just about what he wants, and I do believe they're the best plans I've ever seen."

"My! Some people's children are terribly conceited," Mother laughed.

"Well, they are the best plans," repeated Fred. "After all, they have Nancy's ideas in them and being a woman, she knows just how a home should be. Now, let me think, what did I do with those plans? I think I put them in this closet."

Mother returned to the kitchen. Ellen took a book from the bookcase and sat down to look at it. Her heart was pounding fast. Fred would find the plans gone! Oh, if only she had never taken them! If only she had listened to John and had asked Fred for them! She pretended not to notice as Fred opened the closet and looked on the shelf. He was so tall he could look without even standing on tiptoe.

"That's strange," he muttered as he moved everything on the shelf, and knocked down a few hats. "I'm sure I put them here."

He picked up the hats and put them back, closed the closet door, and then started to search in the drawers of the desk. He looked in all four of them, taking everything out and putting it all back.

Ellen sat watching her big brother try to find something that wasn't there. She felt very uncomfortable and very sorry. She wanted to tell him, but she didn't know how.

Then she felt Fred looking at her. Would he ask her if she had seen his drawings? She stared at her open book, reading the same sentence over and over again. She was beginning to feel sick. "Please don't let him ask me—please don't let him ask me," she kept saying to herself.

"Ellen!" began Fred.

Just then Mother entered the living room. "They must be around the house somewhere," she said. "They couldn't just walk away."

"Well, I don't know," replied Fred. "With a kid in the house, anything can happen, and usually does."

"Now, that isn't fair," Mother defended Ellen.

"Whenever anything is missing, you blame poor little
. . . Why, Ellen, what's the matter?"

Ellen had suddenly started to cough very hard. "Drink!
Gotta get a drink!" She ran to the kitchen.

Mother went on talking to Fred. "Can't you show
Mr. Luse your new plans instead?"

"They're not finished yet, and besides they're not as
good as the first ones Nancy and I worked on. And if I
can't show Mr. Luse the plans I told him about, he'll
think I'm a bluff—that I don't really have any plans
at all."

Ellen came back to the living room.

"I don't know where to look next," Fred was saying.
"I guess I'll look for them Saturday when I have the
whole day off. I'll phone Nancy, too. Maybe she'll remember where I put them."

Ellen felt better. But Saturday would be here soon
and then she would have to go all through this again.
She decided to get out of the house to play just as
quickly as she could on Saturday. If she were out of
sight, Fred couldn't ask her anything about the plans.
But poor Fred! The chance he had been hoping for!
The chance to get a job as an architect! It had come
at last, and she had spoiled it for him! Behind the book,
tears were dropping on Ellen's freshly starched blouse.

The sound of Dad's car was heard in the driveway.
Then the front door opened and Dad entered.

"Hello, Dad," called Fred. "Do you know where my
first house plans are?"

"I haven't any idea," answered Dad. "Don't you

know what you did with them?"

"I thought I put them on the closet shelf," declared Fred.

"Come to dinner!" called Mother.

Dad and Fred went to the dining room.

"Ellen!" called Mother.

"I don't want anything to eat," said Ellen. "I'm not hungry."

"What's the matter?" Mother seemed worried. "Are you sick?"

"I don't know. I'm just not hungry."

Dad returned to the living room and put his hand on Ellen's forehead. "She doesn't seem to have a fever."

Ellen pushed his hand away. "Leave me alone," she said.

Fred came in and took Ellen's hand. He tried to be funny and make her laugh. "I'll have to get out your little doctor's kit and go to work on you."

"You're not funny!" Ellen said, pulling her hand away.

"I wonder if she's getting a cold," Mother said.

"Stop talking about me!" Ellen almost yelled. "I'm not sick. I just don't feel well. I just want to go upstairs and lie down. That's all."

Dad and Mother looked quickly at each other. "Do you think we should call the doctor?" they said together.

"Doctor!" Ellen screamed, jumping up. "I don't want a doctor! I'm not sick!"

She ran upstairs, ran into her bedroom, and slammed the door.

Mother started after her, but Dad called her back. "Let's leave her alone for awhile."

"But it's so strange," said Mother. "She's been well all day. Whatever it is, it certainly has come over her all of a sudden."

Ellen, in her room, tried to read, but she couldn't keep her mind on the book. She could only think of how she had hurt Fred. And she had wanted so much to help him. She kicked off her shoes and threw herself down on her bed and began to cry. As she cried, the sick feeling left her, and she fell asleep.

On Saturday, Fred didn't work. A slow all-day rain was falling from a gray sky.

"I'm going to find my drawings if I have to turn this house upside down and shake it," he declared at breakfast.

Ellen, sitting across from Fred, began to eat her pancakes and bacon very fast.

"I asked Nancy, and she said she saw me put them in the closet," Fred said. "Mother, do you think you could have thrown them away by mistake when you were cleaning house?"

"Of course your mother wouldn't throw them away," snapped Dad, as he drank his coffee. "If you'd put your things away carefully, as I do, you'd always be able to find them."

Fred frowned, but said nothing.

Ellen wanted to leave as fast as she could. She stuffed her mouth to empty her plate, and mumbled, "I'm all through. I'm going out to play."

Mother looked at Ellen and covered her eyes with her hand. "Ellen, how could you?"

"It's not easy," remarked Fred, "unless your cheeks are made of rubber, like Ellen's."

"And also, if you don't care how you look!" added Dad.

Ellen sat there, chewing and gulping. When she could speak plainly again, she said, "May I be excused, please?"

"Yes, but don't go out, Ellen. You can't play outdoors in the rain," said Mother.

"Ellen," Dad spoke sharply, "you're not forgetting that you have to help your mother on Saturday mornings, are you?"

"No, Daddy," said Ellen.

"Go upstairs and start making the beds," ordered Mother.

This was all right with Ellen. She would be upstairs working, while Fred was downstairs looking.

As she worked, she could hear Fred moving things around downstairs, looking everywhere for something that wasn't there. When she finished her work, she didn't dare go down. She took a book from her bookcase and sat down by the window to read.

After awhile, Mother called up, "Ellen, what are you doing?"

"Just reading, Mother. I finished the bedrooms."

"Why don't you come down here to read?"

"I don't feel like it now. I'd rather stay up here. It's nice and cozy up here."

Ellen didn't want to be near Fred. He might ask her

and she'd have to tell. If only he wouldn't ask her before Monday!

"El-len!" Mother was calling again. "I want you to go to the store right away. Come down, dear. I have a list ready."

Ellen readily obeyed. Fred was sitting by the bay window in the living room. He looked very, very tired. Mother gave the list and the money to Ellen and went back to the kitchen.

"Now if I can just get past Fred," thought Ellen as she walked quickly and quietly to the closet to get her raincoat.

Suddenly Fred turned. "Ellen! Do you know what happened to the plans Nancy and I drew?"

CHAPTER XVI

Surprise

ELLEN GASPED AND LOOKED at Fred. Here it was at last!

"Well?" snapped Fred.

"I—I—have to hurry—hurry to the store. Mother's waiting."

"Why don't you answer my question?"

"What question?" gulped Ellen.

"Do you know what happened to my drawings?"

"Drawings? Before you said plans."

"Oh, then you did hear my question, didn't you?"

"I—I—er—think you put them on the closet shelf. But I have to hurry now. Mother's waiting."

"Just a minute!" Fred yelled. "I did put them on the closet shelf. But what happened to them after that? Do you know whether anybody moved them from there?"

Ellen felt as if she were dropping through the floor. Fred had asked her. She'd have to tell him now. There was no way out of it. He was staring at her. "Ellen, did you do anything with my drawings? Well, did you?"

She looked up at him, and then looked away. How could she tell him? She stood twisting the little purse in her hands. The list for the store fell to the floor. Fred stooped to pick it up. She couldn't lie to him. He trusted her! But how would she begin to tell him the truth?

"I—uh—that is, we, I mean I . . ."

"You what?" demanded Fred.

The doorbell rang.

"Well . . . ?" Fred kept on.

"Don't you think we'd better see who's at the door?" asked Ellen in a gentle little voice.

"Answer my question!" Fred shouted.

"But somebody's at the door," Ellen's eyes were filling with tears.

"Ellen, you're trying to . . ."

"Sh-h-h!" Mother ran into the living room, her finger to her lips. "Sh-h! Someone's at the door. Do you want them to hear you shout like that?"

"Well, that kid's hiding something!"

Mother went to the door and opened it. Nobody was there. She looked down the street. "It was just the postman," she said. "Here's a letter for you, Fred. From the Model Homes Magazine."

"Throw it away," said Fred. "I can't buy any magazines now."

Ellen gasped. "Model Homes Magazine?"

"That's right," Mother said.

"Oh, Mother," Ellen said in a strange little voice. "Open it. Open it."

"Well, after all," Mother smiled, "even if the letter isn't important, it's addressed to Fred, and we shouldn't open his mail." She handed the letter to Fred.

He took it, saying, "First, I have something to settle with Ellen. Now you listen, young lady . . ."

"Open it! Open it!" Ellen was almost crying.

"Why, Ellen," Mother said, "what in the world is the matter with you? I've never seen you act like this before."

"Make him open that letter," cried Ellen. "If he doesn't open it, I won't tell him anything. And nobody can make me!"

"For goodness sake," said Mother. "Will you be good enough to open that letter at once and put an end to this nonsense?"

Fred tore open the envelope. A green slip of paper fell to the floor. Ellen watched as her brother picked it up and glanced at it. "That's funny!" he said.

Ellen held her breath and waited.

"A check," said Fred, "made out to me. For—for twenty dollars—this must be a mistake."

"Twenty dollars?" asked Ellen. "Oh, no, not twenty dollars! Not just twenty dollars!"

Fred looked at her sharply. "What do you know about this?"

"Read the letter!" Ellen shouted.

Fred began to read. "Dear Mr. Gordon: We are happy to tell you that you have won the first prize of two thousand dollars— What? What's this?" he looked at the check again. "This isn't twenty dollars! It's two thousand dollars!"

"You won! You won!" Ellen shouted, jumping up and down on the sofa.

Fred continued reading the letter. "In our nation-wide contest for the best plans for the ideal one-family house— What are they talking about, anyway?"

Ellen was nearly bursting with joy. "First prize! First prize!" she yelled as she jumped. "I knew you'd win! I knew you'd win!"

Mother looked from Ellen to Fred and back to Ellen. "I wish I knew what this is all about," she said, throwing up her hands.

"I wish I did, too," said Fred. "I didn't send them any plans. There must be some mistake. The prize doesn't really belong to me."

"It does—it does!" Ellen yelled, jumping from the top of the sofa to the floor in front of Fred.

"Ellen," warned Mother, "if you jump on that sofa again, I'll . . ."

Ellen didn't even hear Mother. She was bobbing up and down in front of Fred, shouting, "Ask me the question now, ask me the question now."

"The question?" asked Fred, like a man in a dream. Then a light seemed to go across his face. He grinned, "Ellen, what did you do with my drawings?"

"It was really John's idea," said Ellen. "We read about the contest in a magazine. A prize of two thousand dollars, it said, for the plans of the best house. And there were five other prizes! I heard you say your plans were the best ever, so we knew you'd win something. And you said you didn't want your drawings when you threw them in the closet. John said I should ask you for them, but I wouldn't. Gee, the contest was almost over and I didn't have time to argue with you. So we sent them in as soon as we could. And you won! And now you can marry Nancy right away instead of waiting till you have a long white beard, like you said. . . ."

Fred scooped Ellen into his arms. "Oh, Boy! Did ever a guy have such a kid sister!"

"Fred—I—I can't breathe."

Fred danced around the room with Ellen in his arms. "Two thousand dollars! First prize! Wait till I tell Nancy! Nancy . . . !"

He put Ellen down and ran to the phone. As soon as Nancy answered, he shouted, "Nancy, I just won two thousand dollars! No, I'm not dreaming! It's right here in my hand! See? Well, then, listen. You know our drawings for the house—the ones I was looking for? Well, John and Ellen sent them in to a contest that was almost over, but they got there in time to win first prize! Yes, two thousand dollars! You're coming right over? Well, hurry, Nancy, hurry!"

Fred was grinning when he put the telephone down. "She thinks I'm nutty as a fruitcake," he said.

Mother laughed. "Ellen, those things from the store," she reminded her. "I need them for lunch. You'd better get them right away."

"Right, Mother!"

Ellen bounded out of the house. She ran happily through the rain, all the way to the store. She was too excited to just walk. Everything was so wonderful now! And just about an hour ago she had been so afraid that she had spoiled everything for Fred. And won't Nancy be happy? and John! She ran back to the house with the things for lunch.

Nancy was just inside the door, holding the letter in her hand, listening to Fred. Dad was there, too.

Nancy looked at Ellen. "Oh-h-h, Ellen," she sighed. "This is the happiest day of my life."

Ellen just stood grinning over the bag of groceries. Dad came over and patted her head. He stuck out his chest and said, "Chip off the old block all right. She's got what it takes—my girl has."

"Our girl!" Mother corrected him as she took the bag of groceries from Ellen.

"But, gee," said Ellen. "I couldn't have done it without John."

"I knew as soon as I saw John that he was a smart boy," remarked Dad. "Now we have two things to thank him for. He saved Ellen's life—and now this!"

Fred was saying to Nancy, "Now we can build our little dream house."

"Oh, Fred!" cried Nancy, throwing herself into his arms.

"I'm sure to get that job with Mr. Luse now," he whispered. "And we have two thousand dollars—thanks to Ellen and John." Then he turned to his father. "You can't say anything now against our getting married, can you, Dad?"

"No, Son, there's no longer any reason why you two shouldn't get married. And if you need more money I'll be glad to lend you what I can. Your mother and I are very proud of you."

"We owe it all to Ellen and John," said Fred.

"No, it was your work that won the prize," said Ellen. "I remember how you stayed up late every night working on those drawings."

"But if you and John hadn't mailed them to the magazine," said Nancy. "Oh, Ellen, how shall we ever be able to thank you and John?"

"It was nothing," laughed Ellen. "Now I'm going to write a letter to John and tell him all about everything." Ellen ran upstairs to her room. She got out her best writing paper and began the letter, "dear John, guess what?" And she poured out the whole story to him, and ended it with, "I think you'll be invited to the wedding, too."

CHAPTER XVII

The wedding

Iт was the following June. Ellen and John were in the back yard, playing ball. John had been invited to spend the week with the Gordons for the wedding. After all, didn't John have a big part in making it possible?

"Isn't it wonderful Mr. Morgan gave Fred a steady job?" asked Ellen. "Their house isn't finished yet, but it will be in a month or so. It's being built on a lot that Dad bought for Fred and Nancy as a wedding present. Fred's going to drive out there this afternoon. He'll take us if you want to go. Shall I ask him?"

"Sure," said John. "I like to see new houses being built."

Fred was glad to take them. They drove out to a neat section of new homes, tall elm trees, new sidewalks and new roads. Fred and Nancy's house was set far back from the sidewalk with plenty of space on each side. There was a wide lawn in front—only it wasn't a lawn yet. Just mud. Odd lengths of boards were lying here and there.

They stepped out of the car. "I like that noise," said

John, as they heard the busy hammering and sawing that filled the neighborhood.

"Now you kids be careful," warned Fred. "I don't want muddy feet back in the car."

The good smell of freshly sawed wood filled the air as they entered the new house.

"Watch where you step. All the floors aren't in yet," called Fred. "There are only ladders where stairs are going to be."

"Hello, Mr. Gordon," said a man whom Ellen thought must be the builder. He and Fred began to talk, and Ellen and John left and went about the house, looking at everything.

"If Fred and Nancy are going to get married this week, where are they going to live till their house is finished?" asked John.

"Well, first they're going on their honeymoon. That will take two weeks, and when they come back they're going to live in an apartment until their house is ready."

At last the wedding day arrived. The Gordon family was up early that morning. Mother remarked that it was going to be a beautiful, clear day. The Clarks must have been up early, too, because Fred was talking with Nancy on the phone for a long time. He had eaten very little for breakfast, and he looked pale. Brownie had lain down at Fred's feet under the breakfast table, instead of Ellen's, this morning. It seemed as if he knew that this was the last time he could play with Fred's shoelaces.

Ellen and John ate with happy excitement. Dad was cheerful, but Mother looked as if she would weep any moment. She talked about how fast the years had gone since Fred was "that high" and how soon it would be when they'd have to part with Ellen, too. Her lower lip trembled a little, and Dad covered her hand with his. Then she smiled and looked cheerful again.

The wedding was to take place at eleven o'clock in the morning. Ellen waited as well as she could for the hours to go by. At last she was seated in the church with John beside her. Nancy's mother had just been seated, and the music of the wedding march began to fill the church. Fred stood at the altar steps, waiting for his bride.

Then the wedding procession started slowly up the aisle. First the pink and blue bridesmaids, and then the maid of honor in pale green. And then, oh then, all in shiny white satin and flowing veil, came the beautiful bride, holding her father's right arm. Ellen had always thought Nancy pretty, but now she seemed to spread beauty all around herself, as she walked toward the tall young man waiting for her at the altar steps.

Fred came forward. Nancy put her bouquet in her left hand, and gave her right hand to Fred, who drew it gently through his arm. They walked to the altar together, the maid of honor and the best man following. The organ stopped playing the wedding march, and Nancy handed her bouquet to her maid of honor. Everything seemed hushed in a holy, pure way. Then began the words that would make them man and wife. John and Ellen listened.

"Dearly beloved. We are gathered together here, in the sight of God, and in the face of this company, to join together this man and this woman in holy matrimony; which is an honorable estate, one which is not to be entered into lightly. . . ."

Ellen couldn't possibly remember it all. And then she heard Fred's voice.

"I, Fred, take thee, Nancy, to be my wedded wife, to have and to hold, from this day forward, for better or for worse, for richer or for poorer, in sickness and in health, to love and to cherish, until death do us part."

Then Nancy, with her hand in Fred's, spoke the same promise.

Now the wedding ring received its blessing: "Bless, Oh Lord, this ring, that he who gives it and she who wears it may abide in Thy peace, and continue in Thy favor until their life's end."

Fred then placed the ring on the third finger of Nancy's left hand.

"With this ring I thee wed, and with all my worldly goods I thee endow."

The gentle voices filled the church like soft music. Grown-up ladies touched their eyes with pretty handkerchiefs. They must be crying, thought Ellen, and wondered why. How could anyone want to cry at so wonderful a thing as a wedding?

And then began the last words: "Those whom God hath joined together, let no man put asunder. . . .

"I now pronounce you man and wife."

The organ started to play again. Nancy took Fred's arm and together they walked down the aisle to the front of the church. There Fred took his wife in his arms and kissed her.

Friends and relatives crowded around them. They kissed the bride, shook the groom's hand, and wished them happiness.

Fred and Nancy ran down the steps of the church in a shower of rice. They got into their car which had been gaily decorated with colored paper, a "Just Married" sign, and old shoes.

At the wedding reception there were many good things to eat, and Ellen and John had great fun. Nancy cut the wedding cake, and she and Fred shared the first slice together. This meant that from now on they would share all things in life, good or bad, together.

Fred and Nancy received many beautiful gifts which Ellen loved to look at. There were all sorts of things that they would use in their new home when it was finished.

Later, Fred and Nancy appeared in traveling clothes and said good-bye to all their guests. Nancy kissed her new mother and father, and Ellen, now her sister-in-law. Fred went over to Mr. and Mrs. Clark and greeted them as his new mother and father. Dad and Mother gave a last hug to Fred and his wife, and then the newlyweds got into their car and were off on their honeymoon.

CHAPTER XVIII

A nephew arrives

ARE YOU READY, Ellen?"

"I'm ready. I'm waiting for you."

"All right, dear. Is the car out?" Mother fastened her coat and put her hands into her muff.

Mother, Dad and Ellen got into the car. "Drive carefully," said Mother. "The snow is slippery."

"I have chains on the tires, and most of the roads have been cleared," Dad replied. "Don't worry."

Ellen leaned forward from the back seat, and held a pretty valentine in front of Mother. "See what I made for Nancy and Fred."

"Why, that's lovely. They'll think it's beautiful." Then she said, "My, but I'm anxious to see the new nursery furniture Nancy told me about over the phone."

"I'll bet it's pretty," exclaimed Ellen. "The last time I visited Fred and Nancy, the nursery room was empty."

Soon the car came to a stop in the drive of a small colonial white house with red shutters, set far back from the street. Trees stood on either side, their branches loaded with snow. A cheerful light shone from the window, making the snow-covered lawn sparkle like diamond dust.

Dad helped Mother and Ellen from the car. The front door opened as they walked up the steps, and a smiling Nancy and Fred stood there to welcome them. Nancy called, "Hello, Mother! Hello, Dad and Ellen!"

"Hi, parents and sister!" grinned Fred.

In another minute they were seated in the large living room. Everything looked bright and new. The pretty bay window, the large fireplace, the shining brass fireplace tools, the colonial wallpaper and lamps—Ellen felt like a girl in a lovely picture. She smoothed her blue velvet dress and sat up very straight.

Nancy looked very happy as she brought in refreshments for her guests.

"I have something for you and Fred," said Ellen, bringing out the valentine.

Fred and Nancy praised it, and then she spoke again. "I have something for someone else, too."

"Someone else?"

"Yes. Someone who isn't here yet."

"Oh!" Nancy understood. She laughed and took the white box tied with white satin ribbon and opened it. Then she held up a pair of tiny, knitted bootees.

"I knitted them myself," said Ellen proudly.

"Oh, they're wonderful—and so soft!" Nancy put them against her cheek. "Where did you get such soft wool, Ellen?"

"I had to shop around for it. I made them white so they'll do for either a boy or a girl. You can put pink or blue ribbons in them after you know."

"And you knitted these all by yourself?" asked Fred.

"Sure," replied Ellen, very pleased with Fred's question. "And didn't drop one stitch either. Bootees are just about the hardest things to knit, too. Lots of kids could have done it though, I guess. But maybe they'd have dropped a lot of stitches."

Fred stuck a finger in each bootee. "You couldn't drop many stitches from these tiny things," he grinned. "You'd have nothing left."

Nancy led them upstairs to show them the nursery. In the room that had been empty were a crib, a bathinette, high chair, play pen and chest of drawers. The wallpaper had Mother Goose pictures all over it. Shelves were built against the wall at one end of the room for baby's toys.

"Gee, it's cute," said Ellen. "I can hardly wait."

"Just four more months," said Nancy. She was wearing a pretty maternity dress. Ellen could see that her tummy had become much larger.

"The baby's growing fast, I guess," said Ellen.

Nancy placed her hand against her side. "Oh, yes," she smiled. "I can feel it moving, too. Would you like to feel it, Ellen?"

She took Ellen's hand and placed it where she could feel soft little movements against her hand. "Do you feel it?"

"Ever so little," Ellen replied. "Oh, there! I felt it that time. That was a pretty hard kick."

"It'll probably be a football hero," chuckled Fred.

"Or a ballet dancer," added Nancy. "We might have a girl, you know."

"Um-m," said Fred. "Well, both would be nice."

"Golly, twins!" Ellen exclaimed. "That'd be terrific!"

After a pleasant evening, Ellen and her parents went home. It had begun to snow again. Snowflakes as big as half dollars were falling softly against the car windows as Dad drove on.

The winter passed. A winter full of sledding and ice-skating, school-work and play.

Spring came again! And again the peach trees were covered with lovely pink blossoms. As the season went on, the petals fell, and then were seen the silky baby peaches wearing their cute little caps.

One evening in the early part of June, the telephone rang in Ellen's home.

"It was Fred," said Mother, as she put down the phone. "He took Nancy to the hospital tonight."

Dad looked up from his newspaper.

Ellen gasped, "Her baby?"

"Yes," replied Mother.

"Are you going, Mother? May I go, too?"

"Oh, no. The doctors and nurses won't let anybody in to see Nancy until after her baby is born. They won't even let Fred in. He'll have to wait outside the delivery room in the hospital."

"Why?"

"Because people might bring in germs that would hurt the little baby. They might have colds, and they might cough or sneeze around the baby."

"Will Fred wait there till it's born?"

"Of course, and he promised to phone us as soon as it arrives."

Mother and Ellen sat down together. Ellen was very thoughtful.

"Mother," she said, "it must be wonderful to have your own little baby."

"Yes, Ellen, it is."

"Mother, could I have one—a baby?"

Mrs. Gordon smiled. "Not until you grow up. Your body has to prepare itself to have a baby. Why, you haven't even menstruated yet."

"What does that mean?"

"When you're older, your body will produce each month a tiny egg. It will go from your ovaries into your womb. And each month your womb will get itself ready for an embryo by making its walls thick. If the egg isn't fertilized by a sperm cell the walls will start to shrink again. Then they'll bleed a little for several days. The bleeding is called menstruation."

"What happens to the blood?"

"It flows from the vagina for a few days. A woman wears a sanitary pad to catch the blood."

"And that happens every month?" asked Ellen.

"Yes, but for the first six months or even a year after you begin, it may not be every month," answered Mother. "But when a woman becomes pregnant, that is, when the egg is fertilized, she stops menstruating, and doesn't start again until after her baby is born."

"What happens to the egg if it is fertilized?"

"It plants itself in the thickened wall of the womb and begins to divide and make many cells. As the baby grows, the womb stretches and gets larger. The place where the egg connects itself to the womb lengthens out into the cord. The embryo—or the baby—is fed through it, as it grows in its bag of liquid."

"How old were you when you menstruated, Mother?"

"I was nearly thirteen, but some girls are as young as ten, and some do not begin until they're seventeen. There's no certain age for it."

Ellen listened with interest. "Some day I'll have my own children, won't I, Mother?"

"Yes, indeed, but not until you've grown up. And not until you've met the man you love enough to marry and have for the father of your children. And of course, you and your husband must have a home ready for the first little baby."

"It's wrong for people to have a baby without getting married, isn't it?"

"Of course it's wrong. A child needs a father and a mother who live together and can take care of him. He needs both parents to love and protect him."

Ellen seemed thoughtful.

"Suppose a little baby were brought into the world by a girl who wasn't married," Mother went on. "How would she take care of it? She couldn't earn the money for the things it needs and take care of it at the same time. And the child would have to grow up without a father and without a home. People have to get married first, and have a home together, and be able to take care of a baby. When they get married, they promise to stay together all the rest of their lives."

"Well, couldn't the girl bring up a baby in her own home?" asked Ellen.

"No, Ellen," answered Mother. "Both parents are needed to bring up a child."

"I hope I meet a man as nice as Fred when I grow up," said Ellen.

After they talked awhile, it was Ellen's bedtime. She kissed Mother and Dad good night and went upstairs.

Suddenly Ellen was awakened from a sound sleep by the alarm clock. Slowly she opened her sleepy eyes. She must have been only dreaming about an alarm clock because it was still black night.

"That's it!" Daddy yelled. She heard him leaping down the stairs. She sat up. That wasn't the alarm clock! It was the telephone! Nancy's baby! Dad was talking excitedly on the phone. She heard him say, "God bless you, Fred, you and your family."

Ellen jumped out of bed and looked at her clock. Half past five! As she ran to the stairs, Dad was coming up.

"It's a boy!" he shouted. "It's a boy!"

Mother came out into the hall. Her eyes were filling with tears. Dad caught her in his arms. "Hello, Grandmother!"

"Grandmother!" she repeated softly. Then she leaned against Daddy and started to cry. He kissed the top of her soft hair and held her close to him. "I'm so happy," she sobbed.

Ellen strutted in the hall, patted herself on the chest, and grinned.

"I'm an aunt! I have a little nephew! Hm-m-m! An aunt, with a little nephew!"

She felt that her place in life had been raised—in fact, she felt quite important. Aunt Ellen! Hm-m! Aunt Ellen!

CHAPTER XIX

Home

THE DAY CAME at last! Mother and Dad were going to take Ellen to see her little nephew!

Her parents were almost ready, but Ellen was too excited to sit still in the living room and wait. She grabbed her straw hat by its ribbons and ran out front.

It was a wonderful summer day. The sky had often been a clear blue before, but never a blue like this. The leaves of the trees had often shone in the sun, but never before had they spangled like this as the summer air sighed against them. And never before had the sun felt so good on Ellen's bare arms and legs.

Mother and Dad came out and they all got into the car. Soon they arrived at Fred and Nancy's home. The front lawn was a rich green and a lawn sprinkler was tossing water high in the air. It fell like a shower of diamonds.

"Everything looks so beautiful today," thought Ellen as she lifted the brass door knocker, once—twice. The door was opened by the beaming father. His dark eyes shone. Ellen felt that if he were any happier he'd burst into sunbeams!

"Come in!" he cried, and they all went into the living room. Nancy came in and welcomed Ellen and her parents. She was wearing a slim-waisted white dress. Ellen noticed that her tummy was now quite flat again.

"I know how anxious Ellen is to see the baby, so let's all go up to his room right away," she said.

"You go first, Ellen," said Mother, stepping aside so Ellen could follow Nancy up the stairs. "Dad and I saw little Charles Frederick at the hospital, but you haven't seen him yet."

"Thanks, Mother." Ellen tiptoed up the stairs. "We'll have to be quiet—he may be sleeping," she warned.

She tiptoed after Nancy into baby's room. There in his crib, cozily tucked beneath a blue blanket, lay Aunty's little nephew, sound asleep. Ellen smiled and put her hands behind her back. She just stood, admiring him. His dark hair turned up all over his head in silky little ducktails. His fingers were plump and pink and half curled into little fists, which he held up over his head as he slept. He had a cute nose, and Ellen noticed how perfect his little ears were.

"Oh-h-h," she whispered, "he's so sweet, and so little."

"Isn't he a darling?" Mother said softly. "He sleeps with his arms up over his head the way you used to, Fred."

"Really?" Fred smiled happily to think that his infant son was already imitating him.

"He has little fingernails," said Ellen. "Such tiny fingers to have fingernails."

"A baby is a wonderful thing, isn't it, Ellen?" Daddy smiled.

"I wish I could touch him, Daddy. He looks so soft and cuddly. May I touch him?"

Dad leaned over and whispered, "Sure, go ahead and touch him if you want to."

Ellen gently placed one finger in the palm of baby's little hand. The small soft fingers curled down on her finger.

Then little Charles Frederick opened his mouth and yawned. After everyone had praised the cuteness of it, he opened his dark eyes—and blinked—at Ellen.

"This is your Aunt Ellen," said Nancy, bending over his crib. Ellen felt a quick flutter of pride. Aunt Ellen!

Nancy looked at her wristwatch. "Why, you woke up just in time for your feeding, didn't you, you little darling?" She turned back the blue cover. Ellen saw that he was wearing the white bootees she had knitted for him. Nancy took him up in her arms and put her cheek lovingly against his silky head as she carried him to the bathinette. Then she laid him down on the canvas top to change his diaper.

"Will you get me a clean diaper from the top drawer of the chest, Ellen?" said Nancy, knowing that Ellen wanted to help.

When she returned with the diaper, Nancy was cleaning the baby with a piece of cotton dipped in baby oil. It smelled sweet and clean in a baby sort of way. Then Nancy put his diaper on him. "If I keep him very clean, he'll never be uncomfortable. They told me in the hospital how to take care of him."

"I wish I knew how to take care of a little baby," Ellen said.

Mother watched Nancy washing the baby. "The years go by so fast," she said. "Why, it seems only yesterday that I was taking care of my children, just as Nancy is taking care of her baby now."

Dad and Fred were standing together at the window, looking out at the garden. "Little Charles is a lucky baby to have such good parents and such a nice home," remarked Dad.

"We hope we'll be able to make him as happy as you and Mother have made Ellen and me," Fred replied. "I hope he'll always come to us whenever he feels he needs a friend, or for help in anything at all, as I always went to you and Mother. It makes a big difference in a fellow's life, you know."

"I'm sure he will, son. Just make him know that he can talk with you about anything—anything at all—and he'll always find a friend in you. Be sure of that!"

Then Fred said, "Dad, how would you like to see my tea roses? They're doing better than I expected."

"That's something I want very much to see. You remember how beetles ate ours when we tried to raise them?" Dad followed Fred from the room.

"Roses are my favorite flower," declared Ellen, looking into the garden. From the window of baby's room could be seen the big yard with its green lawn, its grand old trees, its young shrubs in bloom, its bright flowers.

Nancy held her baby and joined Ellen at the window.

She told her the names of all the flowers she had planted. "And Fred's going to make a playground for Charles in that part of the yard," Nancy pointed to it, "as soon as he's old enough to use it. Swings, and a slide, and a see-saw. And when he's old enough I'll teach him to take care of his own little garden, so he can watch things grow."

Nancy sat down in a rocking chair with her baby in her arms, and unbuttoned the front of her white dress to nurse him. She asked Ellen to hand her a covered jar, which, she said, had water in it that had been freshly boiled that day, and also another covered jar of cotton. With these, she washed the nipples of her rounded breasts. Then Nancy pillowed her baby's head with her arm and put the clean nipple of her breast in his little mouth. He drank his milk contentedly. His mother looked down at him, her face all smiley and curvey with inner joy.

Here was the richest wonder of life—a baby born of the love of one human being for another. Ellen remembered some of the words Fred and Nancy had said at their wedding—"for better, for worse . . . till death do us part."

"You and Fred will always be together now, as long as you live, won't you?" asked Ellen.

"My, what a serious little girl you are," laughed Nancy. "Of course we will."

"Gee-e-e-e!" sighed Ellen.

"Why that long gee-e?" smiled Nancy.

"Oh, nothing—except—people have to be very especially careful about choosing each other when it's for keeps like that."

"Indeed they do," agreed Nancy.

Then Ellen said, "I wish I could be with my cute little nephew a lot. I want so much to help care for him. I could take the bus over every day."

Nancy remembered how much she had loved being with babies when she was Ellen's age, how dull her dolls had seemed afterwards. She saw the memory of it all in Ellen's blue eyes, looking up at hers.

"I was hoping you'd offer to do just that, Ellen. I'll need so much help with this little rascal."

"And who could help better than his own Aunt Ellen?" said the aunt, gazing fondly at her nephew.

The End

CPSIA information can be obtained at www.ICGtesting.com
Printed in the USA
BVOW02s2250110314

347394BV00008B/125/P